# MINE:
## A LOVE STORY

## SCOTT PRUSSING

This is a work of fiction. All the characters or events portrayed in this novel are either fictitious or used fictitiously.

MINE:
A LOVE STORY

Scott Prussing Publishing
1027 Felspar St.
Suite 2
San Diego, CA 92109

ISBN: 0615600999
ISBN-13: 978-0615600994

To everyone who has ever won or lost at love.

# CHAPTER 1

I believe in fairy tales—sort of. I mean, I want to believe. I need to believe. And not just in the standard ones, like Cinderella and Snow White marrying their princes and living happily ever, or Belle's ugly Beast turning into a handsome prince. No, I believe in tales like Romeo and Juliet, too. Only in my version, there's no poison and no knife. Just joyful years together. And lots of cute kids. Pretty cool, huh?

There's a reason I need to believe so strongly. If you spent even a couple of days in my life, with my father and mother, you'd see it. I know they were in love once—I've seen the photos and read their old letters. Probably, they still love each other, in their own weird way. But they fight all the time. And when they're not fighting, they're arguing, and if they're not arguing, they're bickering. Constantly. At each other, back and forth. Pick, pick, pick. I hate it. When it gets too loud, I lock myself in my room and try to drown them out with my guitar. I love that guitar.

This kind of family life has molded me, for sure. I'm the most cautious girl you know. Cautious about what I say, cautious about what I do, cautious about who I let into my life. I'm so cautious no one has ever heard me play my guitar. That's right. Nobody. Except my mom and dad, and they've only heard me through my closed door. I think I play pretty decent, but I'm afraid of the kind of comments I'd get if I played for anyone. That's what happens when you grow up in home filled with so much negativity. I'm kinda shy, too. Shy and insecure—what a winning combination. I finally got on Facebook this year, and I've got all of fourteen friends. And five of those are my cousins. How many eighteen-year-old girls do you know who have only fourteen Facebook friends?

But I'm in a good mood today. Guardedly happy, but happy nonetheless. In just an hour or so, I'll be leaving for school—State U. I'll be living on campus. No more fighting, no more arguing, no more bickering. I hope I get a cool roommate. If I do, maybe I'll even let her hear me play my guitar. Maybe…eventually….

Mom and dad want me to live at home—State's less than twenty-five minutes away, an easy commute. Are you kidding? Live at home? I mean, it's not that I don't I love them. I do. They're my mom and dad, after all. But that doesn't mean I'm going to stay one minute longer than I have to. They're paying my tuition, but I'm paying the room and board—every penny of it. I've been saving for this since I started babysitting when I was twelve, and almost every cent I made working at the gift shop the last two summers and after school went right into my "escape fund." Today, I escape. Hooray!

Right now, I'm digging into a stack of blueberry pancakes mom whipped up in honor of my last breakfast at home. They're fantabulous, topped with real butter and sweet maple syrup. Mom's a really good cook. I think she's hoping the memory of these pancakes will get me back here for more home-cooking sooner rather than later. As another delicious bite slides down my throat, I think maybe it wouldn't be so bad to slip home for an hour or two now and then—at dinner time, of course.

Then dad comes into the kitchen, and I remember why I'm so happy to be leaving.

"How come you never fix a breakfast like this for me?" he asks my mom.

His tone is sort of light-hearted, and I know he's only teasing, but that's how it usually starts. I instinctively reach for the iPod I keep fastened to my belt, but earphones are forbidden at the table, so there's no refuge for me there.

"Oh, Henry," mom replies. "It's Heather's last meal here. I wanted it to be special."

"She'll only be ten miles away," dad grouses. "She knows we'll come get her any time she wants. Heck, she could walk home in a couple of hours if she wanted."

Dad knows I love going for long walks, but that's not the point. Besides, the reason I started taking the walks in the first place was to get away from all this, not to come home.

"And you'd probably make her walk, wouldn't you?" mom counters. "That would be just like you."

And so it begins, again. Since I can't use my iPod, I play music in my head. I've gotten really good at that. One of Taylor Swift's earliest songs, "One Way Ticket," has been my escape anthem for four or five years now, and it automatically fills my brain. She sings about buying a train ticket and seeing how far away she can get. I can't believe how young she sounds, how young she was when she recorded it, on a demo CD yet. Lost in the lyrics and the music, I barely taste my pancakes. Mom and dad's bickering has a way of sucking the joy out of most things, even something as awesome as homemade blueberry pancakes smothered in butter and syrup.

Mom and I are standing beside the driveway, watching dad load my stuff into the back of our Explorer. Our chocolate Lab Sam sits in front of us, watching as well. His tail isn't wagging with its usual vigor, and I wonder if he knows what's happening, that I'm leaving. He's a pretty smart dog. I'm going to miss Sam.

It's a beautiful morning. Warm, but not hot. A gentle breeze carries the scent of mom's rose garden to the driveway. I love the smell of flowers. Roses, honeysuckle, jasmine—you name it. Above us, the narrow contrail of a high-flying jet is streaking through a crystal sky, heading straight for a giant white cloud. Most people would probably think of a missile heading for its target, but I see Cupid's arrow aimed at a waiting heart. I told you I was a romantic.

I've got my long, dark blond hair tied behind my neck, keeping it out the way while I packed and carried my things out. I'm wearing a dark blue Old Navy T-shirt and ripped jeans. Nothing special. The jeans didn't come ripped—they're way too expensive to buy that way. I don't spend much on clothes. Like I said, I've been saving my money for years so I could live on campus. My guitar and iPod are about all I've splurged on, and I consider those necessities, not luxuries. All that scrimping is about to pay off. I used scissors and my hands to rip my jeans, and they look just as good as store bought ones. Better, if you ask me.

Dad is struggling to fit one of my boxes into the back, but mom and I make no move to help him. We've learned that with projects like this, it's best to stay out of his way and let him do everything himself. We helped carry the boxes and suitcases out to the car, but we're letting him load it. My mom has her arm around my back. It feels good. One my other side, I'm holding my guitar case. That feels good, too. No one touches my guitar but me. Not even when it's in the case.

I've read every word the college sent about my dorm and the things I should bring. I made notes of anything I thought was important, and I've got a list of everything I want to take. I checked each item off as I packed it. Cautious girl, being thorough.

There's not all that much stuff. I'll be living in one of the oldest dorms on campus, in a single room with one roommate. I learned the other day her name is Marissa, but that's all I know about her. It would have been nice to live in one of the newer suites with my own bedroom and a couple of roommates, but those are way more expensive, so I chose the cheaper option.

"You haven't told us what courses you decided on for your first semester," mom says.

"Oh, just the usual," I say. "Required stuff—English, algebra, American history. And psychology as an elective. That might be fun." I don't tell her about the special fifth course I signed up for, which I hope will really be fun. She might understand, but dad won't. And I don't want to hear anything about wasting his tuition dollars.

"I'm sure you'll do great in all of them," mom says. "Look how well you did in high school. College is just like high school, except the kids are older."

Ugggh. I hope it's not anything like high school, for more reasons than I care to share with my mom.

Finally, dad is done loading. The cargo area of the Explorer is packed tight.

"All set," he says. "Take a look. A perfect fit, like a giant three dimensional jigsaw puzzle."

Mom and I murmur appropriate praises. I open the back door and Sam jumps inside, excited he's not being left behind. I ease my guitar case onto the seat beside him and climb in. Mom slides into the passenger seat and Dad gets behind the wheel and backs out of the driveway. We're on our way!

In the car, there are no rules against earphones, so I stick mine in before we're even out of our neighborhood. Dad always has the radio set to a Rock and Roll station. I like the music, but the stereo doesn't drown out their bickering like earphones do. Kellie Pickler's "Best Days of Your Life" fills my ears. I can see mom and dad's mouths moving—sometimes both at once—but mercifully, I can barely hear them. If I have to guess, they're arguing about dad's driving. Mom thinks he drives too fast and follows too closely. Which he does. Dad thinks he's the world's greatest driver. He's always saying he should have driven in NASCAR. Says he probably would have if he hadn't gotten married and had a kid so young. Gee, Dad, do you ever think how that makes your kid feel?

Fifteen more minutes and we'll be at school. Thank god. The guy in Kellie's song may already have had the best years of his life, but I'm pretty sure mine are about to start. I sure hope so, anyway.

## CHAPTER 2

We're here! I know it's barely ten miles from home, but it feels like I'm in a whole different city. It's not the distance that matters, it's the separation, the freedom. I can't keep from smiling as dad swings the Explorer through a wide stone gateway onto the campus. He slows down now, meandering along shady lanes, past impressive old brick and stone buildings, many fronted with thick white columns. Some of the buildings sit close to the road; others perch behind lush green lawns or thick hedges. We drive by a row of stately wooden houses that contain administration and faculty offices. It really is a pretty campus.

A few more turns and dad eases to a stop in front of a rectangular four-story brick building. It's barely ten o'clock, and there's only one other car here. Most kids are probably coming from farther away and will take longer to get here. That's good for us, allowing dad to park in the shade of a leafy maple, directly in front of the cement walkway leading up to the front door. That means less distance to lug my stuff, too.

I study the old building. Twisting vines of dark ivy

climb the weathered brick to the bottom of the second-floor windows. The words Thompson Hall are etched into a white triangular frieze above the front entrance. There are plenty of buildings on campus with more charm or character, but I don't care. A small lump forms in my throat. I'm looking at my new home!

"Home, sweet home," mom says as dad switches off the engine.

We all climb out of the car. The new surroundings seem to have brightened Sam's mood as much as mine. His tail wags joyously as he scampers up and down the narrow strip of lush grass between the street and sidewalk, never getting too far from the car, though.

"Come, Sam," I call. He races back to me and I kneel in front of him, scratching him behind both ears. I'd like to think he's feeling my joy, but I think he's probably just excited to be somewhere new. So I guess in a way, he is sharing my joy, because I'm definitely thrilled to be somewhere new.

"Well, let's get started," dad says, pulling up the cargo door.

Mom opens the back door of the Explorer. "In you go, boy," she says to Sam. "I doubt you're allowed inside the dorm. You can guard Heather's stuff while we're inside."

With the windows half down and the shade of the maple to keep things cool, Sam will be fine in the car for a few minutes. He sticks his nose out the window and watches as dad hands mom and me a couple of the smaller boxes. Dad grabs my two heavy suitcases, lifting them easily. We follow him up the walkway. Near the doorway,

I ease ahead of mom and dad and pull the glass door open.

There's a single elevator across a tiled lobby. Mom pushes the up button, and it glows yellow.

"We didn't have an elevator in my dorm back in college," dad says. "Fourth floor, I was. Three years trudging up and down those stairs a dozen times a day. Finally got smart my senior year and moved down to the second floor." He rubs his slightly rounded belly. "Kept me in shape, though."

"I'm on the fourth floor, too," I say. "Room 401."

The elevator arrives with a loud ding, and the metal doors slide open. We step inside and dad drops the suitcases to the floor with a loud thud as the elevator rumbles upward. I hold my breath for a moment, hoping the jolt of the heavy suitcases won't mess up the old elevator. Cautious girl worries about all kinds of things.

We make it to the fourth floor without any problems. Room 401 is directly across from the elevator. Convenient, I think as I retrieve my room key from my pocket. Fingers trembling with excitement, I fumble awkwardly for a few seconds before getting it into the lock. I grin sheepishly at mom and dad before twisting the key and pushing the door open.

I can't believe how happy I feel as I step into the room. My room. Well, mine and Marissa's, anyhow. Mom and dad follow me inside.

The room is pretty much what I expected. It's kind of small—barely bigger than my bedroom at home—and I had that all to myself. The furnishings are simple and practical. The coolest things are the windows. Since it's a corner room, there's one on the far wall and one to the left.

They're arched, Gothic-style, with diamond-shaped lead frames. Almost like a medieval castle. I remember seeing that the bottom three floors had plain rectangular windows, so I'm glad I'm on the fourth floor. The faint scent of bleach from a recent cleaning lingers in the air, so the first thing I do is crank open the windows. Then I survey my new home more closely.

Twin beds rest against the two side walls, which are painted a bluish-green hue, probably called sea-foam or something like that. "Puke green," I'll hear it called disparagingly by a girl down the hall a few days later, but I'm pretty sure that's not the official name. Beyond the beds, mirrored sliding doors front the narrow closets—no walk-ins here. Good thing I don't own a lot of clothes. There's also a pair of four-drawer oak dressers on the far wall, as well as two small desks. A porcelain sink with a mirrored cabinet above it protrudes from one wall. Showers and toilets are communal, down the hall. I'll check them out later, but I'm sure they're not anything fancy. I just hope they keep them clean.

"It's small, yet somehow not cozy," dad says as he puts the suitcases down in the middle of the floor.

"Oh, shush," mom says. "It just needs a few personal touches, that's all."

"Why don't you start unpacking," dad says to me, "while your mother and I go get the rest of your things."

"No, I'll come down with you," I say. "I need to say good-bye to Sam."

The elevator is waiting for us across the hall, another advantage of being one of the first to arrive. Back at the car, I hug Sam good-bye while dad unloads the rest of my stuff.

"I'm going to miss you, Sam. But don't worry, I'll drop by before too long." Sam is worth putting up with my mom and dad for a couple of hours. And who knows, maybe they'll be so happy to see me when I visit they'll stop bickering for a little while. A girl can hope, can't she?

A second trip up the elevator is all we need to get the rest of my stuff to my room.

"Do you need any help unpacking and getting set up?" mom asks.

"No, I'm good. Orientation doesn't start until this afternoon, so I've got lots of time to get settled."

"Okay," mom says. "Call us if you need anything."

Dad pulls a hundred-dollar bill from his wallet and hands it to me, an uncharacteristic piece of generosity, especially since he's against my living on campus in the first place. "For any incidentals you need," he says.

I give him a warm hug, then walk them over to the elevator, where I hug mom while dad holds the doors open, just in case someone calls the elevator from downstairs. Finally, I let go, and mom steps into the car. I'm pretty sure I see tears misting her eyes.

My own eyes feel a bit moist as I cross back into my room and let out a big sigh. I can't believe I'm finally here.

Since I'm the first to arrive, I guess I get to pick which side of the room I want. I choose the side with the window. I'm hoisting a plastic storage box onto a shelf in top of the closet when I hear a female voice behind me.

"Wow, you're really tall."

I *am* tall, and self-conscious about it, too. Almost six feet, I tell people who are impolite enough to ask, though I'm actually six-foot-one. I never wear heels, but I'm still much taller than most girls I meet. I need to hang out with the women's basketball or volleyball teams, I think. If I were more coordinated, maybe I could actually play. But I've never been any good at sports.

I turn around and see a short, dark-haired girl standing just inside the doorway. The tips of her straight, shoulder-length hair are dyed so blond they're almost white. She can't be more than five-three. I find myself hoping this isn't Marissa—how am I going to be best friends with someone so short? I'll feel awkward and gawky all the time. And really I do want to be best friends with my roommate.

"And cute, too," she says after I turn to face her. "Really cute."

I take a closer look, trying to see if there's anything in her face that would belie her words, because I don't think of myself as all that cute. Past history tells me differently. Her face is round and pretty, and she's flashing a bright smile at me. There's a hint of something exotic in her features—maybe a bit of Spanish or American Indian or something. She's got a small glass stud on the right side of her nose. Her dark eyes don't show any guile or insincerity. She's wearing a gray top off one shoulder with "PINK" scrawled diagonally in pink letters across a curvy chest.

I think about my own less sexy shape. A girl's figure is the one place where B's or C's are way better than A's. Oh, well, there's nothing I can do about it. The shirt looks

13

great on her. I don't own any Pink stuff—it's amazing how that one simple word adds twenty or thirty dollars to the price of a shirt. Her jeans are ripped—maybe if she did them herself like me there's hope for us yet. Her shoes are dark gray platforms, at least three inches high, which means she's even shorter than I first thought. Short girls are lucky. They can wear heels and be taller. Tall girls can't do anything to make ourselves shorter. Except sit down.

"Hi," I manage to say. "You're cute, too."

Her smile grows wider. "I am kinda cute, huh?" she says. "But not like you. You're gorgeous."

I don't know what to say to that. If I'm so gorgeous, where are all the guys? A line from a Sara Evans song pops into my head, something about straight haired girls wanting curly hair and brunettes wishing they were blond. Probably all the short girls wish they were tall. I wonder if the built ones wish they were flat. Somehow, I doubt that. Anyhow, I'm pretty sure I look uncomfortable.

"Don't worry," she says, grinning. "I'm not hitting on you or anything. I like guys *way* too much."

"No, no," I say. "I didn't think that. I'm just kind of awkward sometimes. Sorry."

"I'm Marissa," she says, walking toward me. "You must be Heather."

"Yes," I say, extending my hand to shake hello.

She walks right past my hand and envelops me in a tight hug. "Great to meet you, Heather. We are going to have *some* fun this year, Roomie. I just know it."

I have to admit, Marissa does seem like someone who knows how to have fun. That would be very good for me.

14

And with luck, her outgoing personality will pull some attention away from me, which is how I prefer it.

Marissa lets go and steps back. "My brothers are bringing my stuff up," she says. "They're usually a pain in the ass, but they're good for some things."

The elevator dings across the hall, and a moment later, three short, muscular guys trudge into the room carrying Marissa's boxes and suitcases. Two look so much alike they have to be twins, probably three or four years older than Marissa. The third looks like he's still in high school, maybe a junior.

Marissa introduces them. The twins are Jason and Jeremy, and her younger brother is Michael.

"Wow, you've got a hot one here, Sis," Michael says, smiling at me.

I can't help but smile back. I guess I'm cute enough for high school kids, at least.

Marissa cuffs him playfully on the head. "Down boy. My roomie's off limits." She grins. "As if you'd have a chance, anyhow. Heather's way out of your league."

Michael returns his sister's grin. I bet he doesn't have any trouble with girls his age.

"Never hurts to shoot for the stars," he says. He winks at me. "That's how I roll."

Marissa shakes her head and rolls her eyes. "Okay, boys," she says, pushing her brothers toward the door. "Time to go. Thanks for your help. I love you all, but I want to spend some time getting to know my roomie."

We spend the next hour unpacking and talking nonstop—when we aren't laughing, that is. By the end of the hour I feel like I've known Marissa for years. I don't think

I could have asked for a better roommate.

"We are going to have one helluva year, girl," Marissa says. "Who says freshman year has to be difficult?"

*Freshman year. Difficult.* The words echo in my head, bringing back memories of my last freshman year, in high school. And of the last girl I'd felt this kind of connection with. Gaby.

# CHAPTER 3

My thoughts must be showing on my face, because all of a sudden Marissa is staring hard at me, a perplexed look on her face.

"What's the matter, Heather? One minute you're laughing and smiling, now you look like you're gonna cry."

I force my lips into a weak smile. "Sorry. Something you said brought back some memories."

Marissa sits down on her bed, still looking at me. I try to think of what to say next, but I'm not sure how much I want to get into this now. I can't believe I still feel this stuff so strongly, after all these years. I feel like such a jerk.

"Care to share?" she asks. "Sometimes talking helps, you know."

I pace a small circle in the room. What the heck, I think. I might as well give her an idea about who she's going to be rooming with. Besides, I can stop whenever I feel like it, right?

Where to begin?

"When I try to say this out loud, it sounds so stupid,"

I say. "It was four years ago, for chrissakes."

"Hey, don't worry about it," Marissa says. "I'm totally non-judgmental. I've got plenty of my own crap, believe me. And nothing leaves this room, I promise."

"When you said freshman year doesn't have to be difficult, it brought back some memories from high school." I plop down on my bed. "Some of it was pretty rough."

"Yeah, tell me about it. I was a couple of inches under five feet tall freshman year, and I looked like I was twelve." She places her hands under her boobs and lifts them, grinning. "Luckily, I started growing these my sophomore year—and presto, no one thought I was twelve anymore."

I laugh. I'm feeling more comfortable already. I think Marissa is going to understand.

"I was almost five ten freshman year," I say. "And even skinnier than I am now. And awkward…god, how awkward. I always felt like everyone was staring at me."

I lift my feet up onto the bed and wrap my arms around my shins. "Anyhow, the first couple weeks of school were hell. I didn't have any friends, and I got lots of teasing—and worse—especially from some of the girls. They'd pretend to trip, and bump me into the lockers or knock my books out of my hands. I kept wishing I had one of those invisibility cloaks or something. Every time the bell rang to change classes, I'd feel my heart start racing. I really hated the hallways. And as soon as the day ended, I'd be the first one out the door."

"Girls can be worse than guys," Marissa says. "For sure. They kept asking me if I was lost, telling me

18

kindergarten was down the block, where was my baby-sitter, mean stuff like that. At least they didn't physically bully me, though. I think I was too small for that."

The more we talk, the stronger it all comes back to me. Freshman year...

*I'm hurrying down the hallway, keeping close to the edge, my shoulder almost scraping the lockers. This way, if anyone bumps me, I won't hit the lockers very hard. I've got my books clutched tight against my chest. If I can just make it to math class, I'll be safe for another hour. I hate math, but any class is better than being in the halls.*

*I keep my head and eyes down, avoiding any eye contact that might be seen as a threat or a challenge to anyone, looking out through my eyelashes and trying to stay out of everybody's way. For a moment, I think I'm going to make it. But then I see my worst nightmare— Kristin, with her two pals, Brittany and Ashley. They're only freshmen like me, but Kristin has already established herself as a big shot. And for some reason, she's taken an especially strong dislike to me. She's dark-haired and attractive, tall, but not as tall as me. Maybe she doesn't like girls who are taller than her. Maybe she doesn't like blondes. It doesn't really matter why. I've been her target before. It's never fun.*

*The three girls swerve toward my side of the hallway, angling toward me like sharks heading for fresh meat. I can almost hear the score from that shark movie in my head—da-dum, da-dum, da-dum. They're going to hit, and hit hard. I tense my muscles, awaiting the inevitable blow. Suddenly, Ashley trips, her arms flailing as she tries to maintain her balance. She sprawls into Kristin, who staggers sideways, away from me and into Brittany. Kristin just barely manages to remain on her feet, but Brittany is knocked to the floor. I catch a quick glimpse of a field hockey stick pulling back from between Ashley's legs. I look up. The girl holding the stick is tall, maybe three inches shorter than me. Much thicker though. With a head of impossibly tangled black hair that makes mine look almost straight. She's wearing baggy tan cargo pants and a brown sweatshirt with the sleeves cut off short. She grins and winks at me.*

*Kristin takes a quick look back, sizing up her options, but with Brittany still on the floor, she decides not to confront this stick-wielding Amazon. She yanks Brittany to her feet and the three bullies continue down the hall. The hallway echoes with laughter, mostly from older kids who have witnessed the skirmish. A few freshmen girls clap silently, probably girls who have suffered Kristin's bullying themselves. My savior ignores it all and walks up to me, holding out her hand.*

*"Hi, I'm Gabrielle," she says, "but you can call me Gaby."*

*I clasp her hand. "Hi Gaby, I'm Heather. Thanks for that." I shake my head. "I can't believe you did that."*

*"Speak softly, but carry a big stick," she says, laughing. "You looked like you could use a little help. That Kristin is such an a-hole."*

*"Aren't you worried she'll try to get back at you?"*

*"Naahh. Most bullies don't mess with anyone who pushes back. Besides, I have this." She grins and sweeps her stick across the floor. "The funny thing is, I don't even*

*play field hockey. I just figured it might come in handy."*

*I laugh. "Well, I'm glad you brought it. I wish I'd thought of it."*

*"Freshman year ain't easy, if you're not one of the cool kids." Gaby fluffs her mass of dark curls with her hand. "And I'm definitely not one of the cool ones."*

*"Well, you're cool enough for me," I say.*

*"Thanks." She glances down the hallway, but there's no sign of Kristin and her two pals. "They'll probably leave you alone, now that they know you have a friend." For the first time, I see a little uncertainty on her freckled face. "That is, if you want to be friends."*

*I smile at her. "I'd love to. I could really use a friend, as you just saw."*

*She smiles back. "Great. I'll see you in the caf for lunch, then. Okay?"*

*"You bet." It looks like my days of eating alone are behind me, for which I'm very grateful.*

"Gaby and I became great friends really quick," I tell Marissa. "She was one of the funniest girls I've ever known. We didn't have any classes together, but we met between almost every class and ate lunch together every day. We texted each other every night, too."

"I'll see if I can find a field hockey stick somewhere," Marissa jokes, "in case anyone tries messing with you here. You were lucky to make a good friend so quickly," she adds, her tone serious now.

"Believe me, I know." I don't tell her I'm hoping for the same thing now, but her joke about the field hockey stick makes me think we're on the same wavelength. "I was very grateful," I continue. "And to think, I owed it all to Kristin."

"What happened with her?"

"Oh, she stayed a jerk," I say. "She and her whole little clique, who thought the sun shone out of their butts. But she left me alone, which was all that really mattered."

"So, go on with your story," Marissa says.

"Well, I guess the next important thing happened a week or two later." I close my eyes for a moment to picture it better.

*Gaby and I are at lunch, sitting at a table by ourselves. Gaby nudges me with her elbow.*

*"Don't look," she says. "But there are two guys over there watching us."*

*I put my sandwich down and pick up my napkin. "Where?" I ask as I dab at my mouth.*

*"Two rows over, a little to the right. One's got a blue number eighty-six jersey, the other's wearing a black T."*

*I casually scan the room, keeping my eyes moving, and immediately see who she's talking about. The guy in the jersey is pretty cute, kind of lean, with wavy black hair and a dark complexion. His friend is average looking, with a more muscular build. They're older—at least juniors, maybe seniors. They do indeed seem to be looking at us as they chat. I hope they aren't saying anything bad. Maybe they're making fun of Gaby and me, the way we're making fun of other kids. I hope not, though.*

*I look back at them, and jersey guy catches my eye. Busted!*

*He smiles, then turns and says something to his*

22

*friend. The other guy shrugs. They both stand up and begin walking around their table. Jersey guy is tall—he doesn't really look like a football player. Oh my god! They're coming over here!*

*I grab Gaby's arm. "They saw me looking," I say. "I think they're coming over. What do we do?"*

*She follows them with her eyes. "Nothing we can do," she says, "except hope they're not jerks."*

*They stop on the other side of our table. Jersey guy is opposite me; his friend is across from Gaby.*

*"Mind if we join you," jersey guy asks.*

*No words come from my mouth, but Gaby saves the day.*

*"Sure, take a load off," she says. She's such a lady.*

*They sit down.*

*"I'm Brian," jersey guy says.*

*"I'm Jimmy," says the other.*

*Gaby introduces herself, and I finally find my voice enough to tell them my name.*

*"Nice to meet you both," Brian says, but his eyes remain on me. "I haven't seen you girls around. You freshmen?"*

*"Guilty as charged," Gaby replies.*

*"That's cool," Jimmy says. "Most of the girls in our grade are stuck up tight-asses."*

*"Same with some in our class," Gaby replies.*

*"You guys seniors?" I ask.*

*Brian shakes his head. "Juniors."*

*The bell rings, ending lunch. Dang!*

*"Well, back to class," Brian says. "Maybe we'll see you tomorrow."*

*I hope so. They both seem like nice guys.*

*That night, Gaby and I text like maniacs. She thinks Jimmy's cute, and I think the same about Brian. We wonder if they like us. Why else would they have come over? My caution flag is up, though. Careful Heather does not take chances. I will not get my expectations up. I will not move too quickly. I'm not sure I can say the same about Gaby, though. She's pretty much the full throttle type.*

*Brian and Jimmy join us for lunch again the next day and the day after that. They continue to seem like nice guys, and I'm beginning to open up a bit.*

*Brian must sense that I'm becoming more comfortable. "How about a quick walk outside before class?" he asks me.*

*I look at Gaby. She winks at me and nods her approval.*

*I make sure Brian and I walk past Kristin's table, where she's surrounded by her clique. Kristin hasn't bothered me since I started hanging with Gaby, but she still gives me attitude whenever she sees me, like I'm something she needs to scrape off her shoe. I love the look on her face when she sees me with a junior. One who's on the football team, no less. I wish he had his arm around me—that would really bust Kristin—but no way am I really ready for that.*

*It's sunny and warm outside. Brian and I stroll across the wide grass yard behind the school, talking about nothing and everything. I feel like I'm walking on air.*

*Brian glances at his watch. It has to be getting close to the end of lunch period. He seems a little nervous—why,*

*I don't know. I'm the one who should be nervous. He's a junior, for god sakes.*

"Heather, can I ask you something?"

"Sure," I say. "What?"

*He stops walking and turns to face me. I like that I have to look up a bit to look into his eyes.*

"I was, uh, wondering, if…uh…"

*I can't help smiling. He's as nervous as I am. Welcome to the club, Brian.*

"…if maybe you'd like to go out Friday night."

*I'm stunned. I'm screaming "yes" in my head, but nothing is coming out of my mouth. I think Brian is mistaking my shock for reluctance.*

"No big deal," he says. "Something simple. Go for a pizza, maybe. I can't stay out too late. Got a game on Saturday."

*My brain finally engages my tongue. "That'd be great. I'd love to."*

*He smiles, and I feel myself melting a little.*

"Great," he says. "I'll pick you up at seven."

*Now I really am walking on air. I've got a date with a junior!*

## CHAPTER 4

"None of this sounds all that traumatic so far," Marissa says, grinning. "A cool best friend and dating a cool older guy."

I laugh. "No, those were the good parts. I may have minimized the bullying and stuff, especially before I met Gaby. But the next few months were pretty good, for sure."

"I'm guessing there must be some bad stuff still to come?" Marissa says.

"Yeah, there is," I say. "But like I said, it was really good for awhile. My first date with Brian was great. We went for pizza, then sat and talked for hours. We stayed out later than he planned, but he played good the next day, so no big deal. I got in a little trouble for being out too late, but I didn't care. I was so happy—I remember dancing around my room after he dropped me off."

Marissa stands up and begins dancing around the room, her arms held in front of her like she's ballroom dancing with an invisible partner.

"I'm in love," she croons. "I'm sooo in love."

I crack up. "I don't think I looked quite that sick," I

say when I stop laughing. "But who knows, I prob-ably did."

Marissa dances herself back over to her bed and sits down. "Tell me more," she says breathlessly. "Tell me more."

"We went out again the next week. And this time, he kissed me goodnight. My first kiss. Mmmmmm...I felt like I was floating. I was sure I was falling in love. We started seeing each other more and more, sometimes doubling with Gaby and Jimmy, who seemed to be going at least as hot and heavy as we were. After about a month, Brian told me he loved me. I was floating. It all seemed so real—like it was going to last forever."

"So, did you two do it?" Marissa asks.

I blush. I'm always uncomfortable talking about this stuff. "No, we didn't. He wanted to, of course. All guys do, I guess. But I wasn't anywhere near ready." I laugh, remembering the time Brian tried to slide his hands up under my shirt.

"He tried for second base once," I tell Marissa, "and I wondered why he was bothering. I've got little enough up there now, and I had absolutely nothing then. I pinched my elbows down over his hands and asked him what he was doing. There's nothing there, I told him. He smiled and kept his hands where they were. I have to admit, I liked the way they felt against my skin. 'I know,' he says. 'I don't care. Besides, I had to try, or else I might lose my man card.' I wasn't quite sure what he meant by that man card thing, but I guessed it had something to do with Jimmy. I wondered if Jimmy and Gaby had already gone there."

My mood flips from wistfulness to sadness. It was

almost four years ago, but it still makes me sad. And angry, too. Marissa sees it on my face.

"Here comes the bad part, huh?" she asks. "You don't have to talk about it if you don't want to."

I pull myself together. "It's okay," I say. "It was a long time ago. Sometimes it doesn't feel like it, though."

"Did it have something to do with Gaby?"

"How'd you guess that?" I ask, surprised.

"It wasn't hard. You were happy and smiling when you were telling me about Brian trying to cop a feel. Then you mentioned Gaby and Jimmy and your face dropped."

Even though it all happened almost four years ago, it still feels like it was yesterday….

*Gaby and I are sitting on a wooden bench in a park not far from school. It's nearly four o'clock, but we usually hang out for awhile after school before we go home. The guys are at football practice, so this a good time for us to catch up. Football will be ending in a week, so we'll see what happens after that.*

*It's a cold November day, but the sun is shining on our bench, so we're comfortable. I'm wearing my fake suede winter coat and jeans. Gaby's got a heavy dark gray sweatshirt and black cargo pants—I swear, she must own a dozen pair of cargoes. I hardly ever see her in anything else. A bunch of children are laughing and screaming as they scramble around on the playground equipment not too far to our left. Three moms are chatting at a picnic table near the equipment.*

*I can tell that Gaby has something on her mind by the way she's chewing hard on some pink bubblegum, as if the chewing helps her think. I've learned that if I just wait, she'll eventually spit it out—spit out what's bothering her, that is, not the chewing gum.*

*"How far have you and Brian gone?" she asks out of nowhere.*

*I know this must be leading up to something big. Gaby and I have done the usual girl talk about how much we love kissing our guys, but we haven't talked about anything more. Until now.*

*"Just kissing," I say. I can tell she's dis-appointed, so I add, "he tried to feel me up, but I stopped him." I open my coat to display my flat chest before continuing. "He cracked up when I asked him what the point was. There's nothing there. He agreed, but said he had to try or he might lose his man card."*

*Gaby chuckles. "That's one of Jimmy's things. He's always saying he has to do this or he has to do that or they'll take away his man card. At least he hasn't used it to try to get sex. He's straight up about asking for that."*

*"Oh my god—are you guys talking about that already?" It's not really that soon, I know, from a guy's perspective anyhow, but with Brian and me still in the making out stage, I hadn't thought about where Gaby and Jimmy might be. Just because I'm an ultra cautious girl doesn't mean Gaby is. She's a lot more adventurous than me, which is one of the things I like about her, usually.*

*"Yeah, for a couple of weeks," Gaby says. "I kind of want to. And Jimmy is definitely ready. We've done about everything else."*

*My face is getting warm, and it's not from the sun. I'm pretty sure I don't want to know what 'everything else' is. "Uh, really?" is all I can manage to say.*

*Gaby winks at me and grins. "And let me tell you, it all feels really good."*

*She sounds like she's already made her decision, or is very close to it.*

*"He says he loves me. And I love him."*

*What can I say to that? Only what my careful brain would say to me.*

*"It's an awful big step, Gaby. Don't rush it. And whatever you decide, please be careful."*

Marissa is perched on the edge of the bed now, listening intently. I think she's guessed what's coming—part of it, at least.

"One night about two months later, Gaby calls me," I tell her. "She's crying on the phone. She's pregnant, she tells me between sobs. And Jimmy, god damn him, has decided he doesn't want anything to do with her anymore."

"Effin' guys," Marissa says, shaking her head.

"Gaby's mom is real old-fashioned. She can't handle the scandal, so she's sends Gaby to her grandmother's in Chicago before she starts showing. You'd think it was 1960, for chrissakes. Gaby and I talk and text every day, but it's not the same. She's going to give the baby up for adoption, and then she'll be back, she says. It'll be just like old times.

"But it never happens. She keeps the kid—an adorable little girl she just couldn't bear to give up. By this time her mom has separated from her dad and joined them in Chicago. So Gaby stays there. We stay in touch for awhile after, but she's so busy with her kid it just kind of fades away. So there you have it—my strongest memories of freshman year."

"That sucks," Marissa says. "What happened with you and Brian? Did you two ever do it?"

"No way. Not even close." I wonder how much I should reveal. Cautious Heather battles briefly with wanting-to-open-up-completely Heather. "I still haven't done it," I say, finally.

"Really? That's cool," Marissa says. "I've only slept with one guy. Danny. We went out most of senior year. But finish your story. What happened with you and Brian?"

"We didn't last much longer than Gaby and Jimmy."

"How come?"

I shrug. "Bunch of reasons, I guess. He and Jimmy were best buds, and after what Jimmy did to Gaby, I couldn't stand looking at him. But it was more than that. Brian was a nice guy, but we really didn't have that much in common. I realized I was more into the idea of being with an older guy on the football team than I was into Brian himself."

"Welcome to the world of high school," Marissa says. "I'm so glad those days are frickin' over."

"Me, too," I say. "Anyhow, now I'm holding out for real love. I just hope I know it when I find it."

"Maybe it will find you," she says.

"I hope so. Because I sure haven't had much luck looking for it."

But that's another story.

# CHAPTER 5

Thursday afternoon. I'm sitting in my room, playing my guitar. One of the first songs I learned: Shania Twain's "Forever and For Always." I guess I've been a hopeless romantic for a long time.

Marissa is at class, so I've grabbed the chance to play. She still doesn't know I even own a guitar. I keep it in the back of my closet tucked behind my clothes and only take it out when she's not here. She and I are getting along great, though, so I'll probably let her hear me play before long. Part of my "opening up of Heather" project. I'm not great on the guitar, but I'm not bad. It's just a big step for me, playing for someone. Marissa will be the first. She'll love that, I think. At least I know she likes country music, which is what I mostly play, although I'll play almost any kind of love song. I'm such a sap!

Marissa likes lots of different music. We have something playing most of the time we're here, sometimes my stuff, sometimes hers. Some of her stuff I like, some of it I don't get at all. Maybe I'll surprise her and learn to play Pink's "Perfect." It's a long way from country, but it's a catchy tune, and I like the lyrics. I'm not sure how it will sound on an acoustic guitar, though. If nothing else, we'll probably get a laugh out of it.

It's only been four days since we met, but Marissa has been great for me. She's so outgoing and so fun—some of that will just have to rub off on me. I hope. She's already talking about taking me shopping to get a few cool outfits. I told her I don't have much money for clothes, but she says she knows a place where they have good used stuff cheap. She showed me some outfits she got there, and they look really good. I can't wait to see what she picks out for me. I'm a little nervous, though—she definitely dresses for more attention than I'm comfortable with.

School has been pretty good so far, too. My psych professor is really fun—I think he's probably a frustrated comedian. English and history are okay, and math is math. Two semesters of required math, and I'll probably never have to do the stuff again. Won't that be nice!

I glance at the clock. Quarter to four. I've got to head to my final class, the one I didn't tell my mom and dad about. I ease my guitar back into the case and place it carefully into the back of my closet. Then I'm off to class.

I've been looking forward to this one. Vampire Lit. Sounds stupid to offer a class on such a mindless subject, I know, but with the popularity of vampire books and movies in the last few years, more and more schools are doing it. Maybe they think it helps enrollment. This one meets just once a week and is only good for one credit. But hey, a credit is a credit, and this class should be fun. I came late to the Twilight books—like I do to most things, it seems—but I really liked them. Did I mention I'm a hopeless romantic? How could I not get into Bella and

Edward's story? I'm hoping I'll learn about some more romantic tales like that.

The small, amphitheater style classroom is almost full of chattering students. Fifty or sixty kids, I guess. I'm not surprised at the crowd. The chance to earn a credit for reading about vampires is too good to pass up for many kids. I'm also not surprised to see the class is at least eighty percent female. Not good odds, but I'm not here to meet a guy—I've got other classes for that. I find a seat in the second row from the top, next to a black-haired girl who is busily pecking away at her laptop. The seat on my other side is empty. Maybe I'll get lucky and it'll stay that way, giving me some extra room.

The professor walks across the small stage in front of the room to a wooden lectern. His thin frame is stooped with age, but he moves confidently, belying his frail appearance. Long white hair hangs limply from his head onto his shoulders, the color a sharp contrast to his rumpled black suit. His black Converse hi-top sneaks don't go with the suit, but he looks like the kind of man who doesn't care.

He's not at all what I expected. I thought this class would be taught by someone young and hip. This guy looks like he could have been around when the original Dracula was written, whenever that was. Hey, maybe he's a vampire himself!

He stands behind the lectern, waiting. The room quiets.

"Welcome to English 131," he says, his deep voice carrying easily through the room. "Vampire Literature. I trust you are all in the right place."

From my seat near the top, I can see almost all of the students. Nobody moves, so I guess everyone is where they're supposed to be.

"As I'm sure you've all guessed by now," the professor says, "I'm Dr. Simpson. "And this handsome young fellow"—he indicates a young man in his mid-twenties wearing a brown sweater and dark tie sitting on a folding chair near the corner of the stage—"is Mr. Randolph, my teaching assistant. I prefer to call him Renfield."

The remark brings laughter from a few kids. The rest—including me—don't get the joke.

Dr. Simpson smiles. "A poor joke, I know, but one that amuses me. I can see that most of you don't get it. Don't worry, by the time we're done, you will."

He shuffles out from behind the lectern to the front of the dais. "Let's take a little poll, see where we are," he says. "By a show of hands, how many of you have read Bram Stoker's *Dracula*?"

Only a few hands go up. I make a quick count. Seven. Five of them are guys. My hand stays down.

"About what I expected," Professor Simpson says. "Okay, another show of hands. How many of you have read *Twilight*?"

This time, I'm looking down onto a sea of hands. I notice not too many of them are guys, though. It figures. Guys have no heart. Blood and guts, they like; romance and passion, not so much. Maybe that's why I haven't had a real boyfriend since Brian. I've been hoping maybe college guys will be different, but maybe not. Oh, well.

"No surprise there, either," Dr. Simpson says. "That's

35

going to save most of you a bunch of reading."

I smile. Coming late to *Twilight* is definitely going to save me some reading. I can recall everything in it pretty clearly.

"Our main focus this semester," Dr. Simpson continues, "will be to be to trace the changes in vampires literature from the beginning to the present. To do this, we'll focus on four books. We'll begin with *Dracula*, the book that started the whole thing. Then we'll move on to *Interview with the Vampire*, by Anne Rice, which created the first boom in modern vampire popularity, back in the seventies. Then *Twilight*, which is pretty much responsible for the current vampire craze. We'll finish with a new book, *Breathless*, by Scott Prussing, which breathes some much needed new life into what has become a very overworked genre."

The only "Breathless" I know is a Taylor Swift song, and that has nothing to do with vampires. But if the book is even half as good as *Twilight*, I'm going to enjoy reading it.

Suddenly, a body plops down into the empty seat beside me. It's a guy, wearing a brown, long-sleeved waffle-knit shirt. I check him out through the corner of my eye. He seems tall—sitting, at least, his head is level with mine—and his light brown hair is stylishly messy, held that way with mousse, I think. His profile is sharp and even. All in all, he's pretty cute.

He might just be a late arrival, but I think I saw him earlier, on the other side of the room. This new seat is no closer to the professor, so he's either moved to get away from someone, or to get closer to someone. Could it be me? Or the girl on the other side of him? She's pretty cute. His eyes are fixed forward, giving no clue. I can't see what color they are without being obvious, and there's no way I'm going to be obvious. I hope they're blue, though.

I turn my attention back to Dr. Simpson, but I can't help sneaking a glance to my right every now and then. One time, I think I see the guy's eyes flicking away from me, but I can't be sure. I spend the rest of class with my attention divided between the professor and trying to think of something to say to the guy beside me. Maybe not during class, but as soon as it's over. So far, everything I've thought of sounds lame. Marissa, where are you when I need you! I'm sooo not good at this stuff.

Finally, Dr. Simpson brings the class to a close. It was pretty interesting. I'm definitely going to enjoy this course. I still haven't thought of a way to start a conversation with the guy next to me, so I guess I'll let him make the first move, if there's going to be one. I think my mom would approve of that, but I'm pretty sure Marissa will get on my case about it.

Anyhow, the choice is taken out of my hands when the girl on the other side of him says something to him. I couldn't hear what, but he replies and now they're talking. Oh, well. You snooze, you lose, I guess. He probably moved to his new seat to be next to her, anyway.

I turn and make my way in the other direction out to the aisle.

## CHAPTER 6

"**W**hat do you mean you couldn't think of anything to say?" Marissa asks when I finish telling her about the guy in vampire class. "Say anything. Say red, blue, green, black—it doesn't matter. Guys love it when a pretty girl starts the conversation. It takes the pressure off them. They don't care what you say. Heck, most of the time they're too busy checking you out to listen to what you said, anyhow."

She's sitting at her desk. I'm perched on the edge of my bed.

"I'm pretty sure the other girl didn't say red, blue, green, black," I say defensively.

Marissa chuckles. "No, probably not. But the point is, it doesn't matter what she said. She said something, and then they were talking. That's how easy it is. Now you'll never know if he moved to be next to you or next to her."

I sigh. "I've never been any good with this kind of stuff."

"Well, you've got me coaching you now," Marissa says, grinning. "And I'm *very* good at it."

She gets up and sits beside me on the bed. "The first

thing we gotta do is get you a new outfit or two. Hunting outfits, I call them. You got any leggings? They'd look great on you."

*Hunting outfits*? That is so not me. I wonder if I'm going to regret this. I usually only wear my leggings to the gym.

"Yeah. I've got black ones and gray ones."

"Cool. With your legs, leggings will be hot." Marissa gets up and begins pawing through my closet. "Let's see what you've got that we can pair 'em with."

She takes a couple things out and holds them up for a better look, but always puts them back. I guess nothing's quite right, in her mind, at least.

"Hey, what's this?" She tips my guitar case forward. "I didn't know you played."

Damn! I'd completely forgotten about my guitar.

"Yeah, I play a little," I say, trying hard to sound nonchalant.

"Cool. Will you play something for me? I love guitar."

I feel my heart begin to race. I'd been planning on letting Marissa hear me play eventually, but hadn't thought it would be this soon.

"On one condition," I say. "I don't usually play for other people." I don't want to say I've *never* played for anyone. That would sound way too serious and way to lame. "So you can't tell any of the other girls I play, okay?"

"Deal."

She pulls the case out of the closet and hands it to me. I put it on the bed and take my guitar out, then sit down and begin strumming the strings. Marissa sits across from me, on her bed.

I'm pretty nervous, so I begin playing a song I've played for years, Taylor Swift's "Teardrops on My Guitar." Part way through, I begin to sing.

"Wow, you're pretty good," Marissa says when I finish. "But in my experience, that wishing star stuff in the song seldom works." She grins. "Now hunting outfits, on the other hand...."

"Okay. Okay. I get your point. I'll let you put something together for me. I don't promise I'll wear it outside the room, though."

"Don't worry, you'll love it. You got any classes tomorrow afternoon?"

"Nope," I say. Like most kids, I avoided taking any classes that meet on Friday afternoons.

"Great. Then you and I are going shopping to-morrow. We'll go to that resale place I told you about."

Marissa and I are in The Buff, a resale clothing store on the edge of campus. The place isn't very big, but it's packed—and I mean packed—with all kinds of stuff. There's barely room to squeeze down the aisles between the racks of clothing. A lot of the clothes are pretty wild—not my kind of thing at all—but I can see why Marissa shops here. Two of the walls are lined floor to ceiling with wooden shelves. The shelves on one wall are filled with jeans, the other with sweatshirts and sweaters. The place smells faintly of burned incense. Lady Gaga's "Edge of Glory" is thumping in the background. I'm not much of a Gaga fan, but I can see why a store like this would play that kind of music.

A half-dozen other kids are rummaging through the store in search of fashion treasure. I'm mostly a bystander, watching Marissa paw through the racks looking for tops for me to wear over my black leggings, which I'm wearing under my jeans. She's already found a long sleeve gray silk shirt with pointed tails that she likes. It's in great condition—I can't believe it's only nine bucks. I've got it draped over my arm while she continues her search for more goodies.

"Take this one, too," Marissa says, handing me burgundy cotton shirt with the same long, pointed tails as the gray one.

I'm sensing a theme here. But so far, nothing she's chosen is out of my comfort zone, for which I'm very grateful, especially considering some of the other stuff I've seen in here. Of course, my leggings are still *under* my jeans.

"Hey, this is cool," she says, showing me a short-sleeve gray shirt with white skulls and purple hearts leading diagonally down the front to a frayed edge.

What is she thinking? That shirt is definitely not my style. No way am I getting that.

"It looks kind of small," I say.

"Not for you, silly. I know it's not your kinda thing. It's for me."

I breathe a sigh of relief.

"C'mon," she says as she spins and heads toward the wall of sweatshirts and sweaters. "Let's get you one more top, and then we'll look for some cool boots."

*Boots*? Who said anything about boots? I'm a

sneakers girl, and flats. I follow Marissa dutifully across the store. It doesn't take her long to find what she's looking for.

"This'll be great when the weather turns cooler," she says, handing me a light, ivory-colored knit sweater with cable stitching.

So far, so good. I like all three of the things she's picked out for me.

"Now, if we can just find the right boots," Marissa says. She looks down at my feet and grins. "Luckily, your feet don't look *too* big. What size are you?"

"Eight and a half," I say. As tall as I am, I guess I should be grateful my feet aren't any bigger.

Marissa leads me to the back of the store, where there are rows and rows of shoes and boots resting on metal shelves, arranged by sizes. She grabs a pair of dark gray, calf-high suede boots.

"Perfect!" she exclaims. "Exactly what I was hoping for. They're in pretty good shape, too."

She holds them out to me. I see a few scuffs in the suede, but they really are in pretty good shape. But what I like best is they have no heels.

"Okay," Marissa says. "Time to see how everything looks on you."

We thread our way to a row of dressing booths fronted by long purple curtains. Marissa hands me the boots.

"In you go, Roomie. Try the gray shirt first."

Taylor Swift is singing "Love Story" as I duck behind the curtain. I love that song and hope it's a good omen about my new clothes. I hang the shirts and sweater on plastic hooks and drop the boots onto a narrow wooden bench. I'm both nervous and excited as I pull off my jeans and sit down to put the boots on. My feet slip easily into them. They're really comfortable, and even better, I don't feel any taller than normal in them.

I put on the gray shirt and check myself out in the mirror. Not a whole lot of light filters in from the top of the dressing booth, so I can't get the full effect of the outfit. The points of the shirt's tails reach to mid-thigh, covering my butt, but barely. The inverted V's on the side show an awful lot of my hips—more than I'm comfortable with, really—but I know I need to get at least a little out of my comfort zone. I suck in a deep breath and step outside the curtain, into the light.

"Wow! You look hot!" Marissa tells me. "That outfit looks even better than I expected. The boots are perfect."

I do a slow pirouette in front of the outside mirror, twisting my neck to examine myself from all angles. The boots and tight leggings draw attention to my legs, which I've always thought are my best feature. The shirt threatens to reveal more of my butt than I want, but it's not like I'm naked underneath. Heck, I've seen lots of girls wearing leggings with shirts that don't even cover their butts, so my outfit is tame by comparison. Still, the overall effect of the combination is a bit provocative, which is exactly what Marissa wants. It's certainly not an outfit I'd wear to class, but it should be great for a party or something. I take a last look at myself and smile. For the first time in my life, I actually feel sexy!

"I like it," I say.

"You should," Marissa says. "You look great. Go try

on the other shirt."

We both agree the burgundy shirt doesn't look quite as good as the gray one, probably because the cotton doesn't hang as well as the silk. But the sweater works great. It reaches just below my butt, like a very short skirt. I buy the gray shirt, the sweater and the boots, all for under thirty-five dollars. Marissa gets the shirt with the skulls and hearts. She wants me to wear the boots, leggings and shirt home from the store, but I tell her no way. This is not a daytime walk around campus outfit—not in my mind, anyhow. I leave the store dressed the same way I entered it, except that my leggings are now in the shopping bag instead of under my jeans.

We head down the block. Near the corner, I stop and grab Marissa by the arm.

"Oh my god!" I say.

"What?" Marissa asks, looking around and not seeing anything that should cause such an outburst. "What?"

"Over there," I say. "On the corner. Waiting for the light to change. It's the guy I told you about. From my vampire class."

Marissa looks at me a little funny. Okay, maybe I've overreacted just a bit. She checks him out. He's wearing tight black jeans, black and white checked sneakers and a vertical striped purple, gray and white button shirt untucked over the jeans.

"He's cute," she says. "Go say hi."

"I can't," I protest. Cautious girl does not walk up to guys and say hi, even if they are cute. Especially if they're cute. "I don't know what to say."

"Well, you'd better think of something," she says,

and shoves me toward him.

I stumble to a stop just a few feet from him. He turns and looks at me. His eyes *are* blue, like I'd hoped. Bright blue and flecked with green, like a lake on a sunny summer day. I realize I have to look up to look into his eyes. He's at least two inches taller than me, which is great.

*Say something, please* I scream at him in my head, but he just looks at me, waiting. I struggle to come up with something clever to say, but my mind is blank. I have to say something, or he'll think I'm an idiot.

"Red, blue, green, black," I blurt, hating myself the instant the words leave my mouth. Now he *knows* I'm an idiot. I wish a hole would open in the sidewalk and swallow me.

He looks at me like I'm speaking Greek. Marissa, I'm going to kill you!

The light turns green. I'm sure I've blown any chance I had, but he makes no move to cross. I think I see the barest glimmer of a smile on his lips.

"Orange, yellow, purple, white," he says.

We look at each other for another moment, and then all of a sudden we're both laughing.

"I'm Chris," he says finally. "What was that red, blue and green stuff all about?"

I blush. "Sorry about that. I'm Heather. My friend told me to say anything," I explain. "She said guys don't care what girls say, as long as we say something to start the conversation. She used 'red, blue, green, black' as an example, and when she shoved me toward you, that's the only thing I could think of to say."

45

"Your friend shoved you?" he asks skeptically.

"Yeah, she did." I turn to point to Marissa, but she's disappeared. I'm on my own.

Chris grins. "Is this friend an imaginary friend?" he asks teasingly.

Now I'm really embarrassed. I must be making quite an impression. First the color thing, and now I'm talking about someone who isn't there. He's going to think I escaped from the local asylum. I wish I was wearing my new outfit. Maybe then he wouldn't notice what a dope I am.

"She was just here," I say lamely. "She knows I'm a little shy, so she pushed me toward you to get me to say hi. She must have ducked into one of the stores."

"Sure she did," he says, still smiling. He seems to be enjoying my discomfort. He lets me suffer for another moment before continuing. "Actually, a girl went into that store over there a moment ago. Short, with dark hair, blond at the tips?"

"Yeah, that's her." I'm sooo relieved. At least he knows I wasn't making the whole thing up. Now if I could just take back red, blue, green, black….

"You're in my vampire lit class," he says. "I sat next to you yesterday."

My heart jumps. He remembers! I tell myself to calm down. Of course he remembers. It was only yesterday.

"I sat there on purpose," he says. "I thought you were one of the cutest girls in class." He grins again. "The cutest with an empty seat next to her, anyway."

I laugh. I like his sense of humor.

"I wanted to talk to you after class," he says, "but that

other chick started talking to me. By the time I got rid of her, you were gone."

I look into his eyes, trying to see if he's still teasing. His eyes are even prettier close-up. The green flecks seem to be floating in the blue. He seems sincere, but I'm not going to commit myself.

"Yeah, I bet you were totally bummed," I say, smiling and keeping my tone light. "A cute girl wanting to talk to you. Guys must hate that."

He laughs. "Well, not usually. But I really did want to talk to you. This is way better, though. If we'd talked after class, I'd probably never have known about your fascination with colors. Now we'll have a great story to tell our grandchildren."

*Whoa! Grandchildren?* This guy is smooooth. Cautious girl better be extra careful here!

"More like a story you'll tell the guys back at the dorm," I say. "About this crazy chick who came up to you and started spouting off colors."

"Naaah, I'll tell the guys in the dorm you walked up to me and started talking dirty. They'll like that story much better."

We both laugh. He's kidding—I hope!

"Do you think your friend wants you to wait for her?" he asks. "Or would it be okay if I walked you back?"

Are you kidding, I think to myself. She'd *love* it if you walked me back. But no way am I going to tell him that. Let's see if he can take as well as he gives.

"I don't think she'd mind," I say. "But how do you know *I* want to walk back with you?"

"Ouch," he says. He makes an exaggerated bow.

"Fair lady, would you kindly allow me the pleasure of walking you home?"

I smile. "Well, when you put it like that, how can a girl refuse?"

I have no idea what I'm getting myself into.

## CHAPTER 7

Chris nods toward my shopping bag. "Can I carry that for you?"

Uh, oh. Funny *and* a gentleman. And did I men-tion he's cute, too?

"Sure," I say. I hand him the bag.

He grabs it by the handles, and then pretends it's so heavy it pulls his arm down to the ground. "What have you got in here?" he asks. "I didn't know The Buff sold weights."

"Ha, ha. Very funny," I say as he lifts the bag back off the sidewalk. "I bought a shirt, a sweater and a pair of boots."

"Boots, huh?" He gives my legs a long, playfully leering look. "Boots would look good on you. What kind did you get?"

"Oh, nothing special," I say matter-of-factly as I begin walking. Chris falls into step beside me. "Just a pair of knee high black leathers." I pause for effect. "With six-inch stilettos. They'll go great with my leather hot pants."

Chris stops abruptly. I wish I had my cell out, so I could snap a picture of his face. After a moment, he realizes I'm messing with him, and he grins.

"Better be careful where you wear that combo," he says. "Guys'll get whiplash if you walk past them in hot pants and six-inch heels."

I smile. "Whiplash? From little ol' me?"

He laughs, and makes a show of moving his eyes slowly from my face all the way down to my feet. "Either that, or you'll get arrested for soliciting."

Did I mention he's funny? We resume walking.

"So, are you a freshman or sophomore?" he asks.

"Just a freshman," I say.

I hope that's okay. Chris seems older.

"Cool. Welcome to State."

"Thanks. What about you?"

"Sophomore."

"So, what got you to take a class like Vampire Lit?" I ask. "You got a thing for vampires?"

"Naahh…." The flecks in his eyes seem to twinkle. "I just figured it'd be an easy credit. Got to grab 'em where you can."

"And I bet it didn't hurt that the class is mostly girls, either."

He looks at me all innocent like. "Is it really? I didn't notice."

"Yeah, right," I say, laughing. "Says the guy who told me he was looking for a seat next to a cute girl."

He laughs. "Well, like I said, you've got to grab 'em where you can. But really, the easy credit was the draw. The other is just a bonus."

He gives me another once-over with his eyes. "A very nice bonus, I have to say."

I feel myself blushing. I don't know how to reply to that. Luckily, Chris takes me off the hook.

"What about you?" he asks. "Are you one of those vampire fanatics?"

"No, not really. I'm a sucker for love stories, though."

"I'm glad to hear you're not a vampire freak. I'm getting so tired of Team Edward or Team Jacob—all that crap."

"I read the Twilight books last year," I admit. "I liked them, but it was more about the romance and passion than the vampire stuff. I figured they'd be part of this class, so that would save me some reading. That book *Breathless* the professor talked about sounds really good, too." I smile. "But getting a credit for something that sounded fun and easy was the main thing."

"Can't argue with that," Chris says.

He pauses for a moment. I can tell he's thinking—I bet he doesn't know he's biting his lip. He looks like he's about to get serious.

"So, Heather," he asks finally, "is there some lucky guy from high school you go home to on the weekends?"

His question catches me so off guard I almost miss a step. It's a good thing I don't wear heels—I'm sure I would have tripped.

"No," I say. "Just my dog, and he doesn't need to see me every week. What about you? You got a girl-friend?"

He shakes his head. "Not anymore. I just broke up with her."

Uh, oh. A rebound. Be careful, girl! Maybe that's why he seems so interested. I definitely don't want to get involved with anything like that.

"I'm sorry to hear that," I say. I really am sorry to hear it—not to hear that he's single, but that it happened recently. "When did you two break up?"

"About ten minutes ago," he says. "When this cute girl started talking colors at me." He tries to keep a straight face, but his mouth stretches into a grin.

"Stop it!" I say, but I can't help laughing.

"Actually, we broke up back in June."

I do a quick calculation. Three months. Not bad.

"How come? If you don't mind me asking."

"Naahh, I don't mind," he says. He doesn't look troubled at all. I wonder if that's a good thing or a bad thing. "She said I was too sweet," he continues.

"Really?" I definitely did not expect to hear that. Maybe she was one of those girls who like bad boys. Lots of girls do.

"And too funny."

Oh, he's kidding again. "Yeah, right," I say. "I think you've been dreaming, Chris."

"And too good in bed."

I crack up. "Now I know you're dreaming. Were you too rich and too smart, too?"

He laughs. "Hey, were you listening when she broke up with me?"

Now we're both laughing. I haven't had this much fun in a long time. Marissa and I laugh a lot, but it's different with a guy.

We keep walking. Chris is really easy to talk to. And our few silences are comfortable, too, which is not something I'm used to. Silences at home are usually just the prelude to an explosion. I like this much better.

We reach my dorm waaay too quickly.

I'm sitting on my bed, strumming my guitar. Not playing anything, really, just fooling around. I got it out as soon as I got upstairs, didn't even take my new clothes out of the bag, which is still sitting on the floor. I like the weight of the guitar on my lap, the feel of the strings beneath my fingers. Playing the guitar helps slow my mind when it's racing. And believe me, it's racing along pretty good right now.

The door swings open and Marissa comes bust-ling through the doorway. She tosses her bag onto her bed and sits down next to me.

"So, how'd it go?" she asks.

"You mean after you shoved me at him?" I say, trying to sound stern.

She grins. "Yeah, then."

"And after I blurted 'red, blue, green, black?'"

Marissa's hands fly to her cheeks. "You didn't!"

I strum a chord on my guitar. "Yep, I did. Thanks to you."

Marissa tries to stifle a laugh. She's only partially successful.

"What did he say to that?"

"He didn't say anything for a couple of seconds. I thought I was going to die of embarrassment. Then he said 'orange, yellow, purple, white.'"

"No way!" She's full out laughing now. "That's too funny," she says finally. "Too funny."

I smile. "He is pretty funny, I have to say. He told me his last girlfriend broke up with him because he was too

53

funny."

"Really?"

"Yeah. And too sweet, and too good in bed."

She laughs again. "He does sound funny."

"And since you disappeared on me, he walked me home."

She's beaming now, obviously very pleased with the success of her scheme. "Just trying to help," she says. "No need to thank me.

"Ha, ha. Don't worry, I won't."

"I told you it doesn't matter what you say to guys, as long as you say something. Who would have thought red, blue, green, black was such a good pick up line? Maybe I'll try it next time I see a guy I like."

"Oh, and did I mention he asked me out?" I ask nonchalantly.

Marissa jumps up off the bed. "No way! When?"

"Tomorrow night." I casually strum a couple more chords. "I told him I'd think about it."

Her jaw drops and her eyes get wide. Her face reminds me of a poster of a famous painting I saw. It's called "The Scream" or something like that.

"You did not! Tell me you didn't say that."

"Why not?" I ask innocently. "I didn't want to rush into anything. He could be an axe murderer or something."

Marissa digs her fingers into her hair. "What am I going to do with you?" she says, shaking her head. "I can't believe you didn't say yes."

I can't keep the grin off my face any longer. Marissa realizes I've been playing her.

"Of course I said yes," I say. "What did you think?

He's really nice."

She sits back down on the bed and puts her hand on my shoulder. "I'm impressed, Roomie. Most girls have to actually *wear* their hunting outfit to catch a guy's interest. All you had to do was carry yours in a bag."

## CHAPTER 8

**I**'m sitting alone in my room, doing nothing. Marissa is gone for the weekend. It's her younger sister's birthday today and they're having a big party for her. My first weekend away at college, and my roommate is gone. I could have gone home, too, but the point of living on campus is to NOT go home, at least not too often. My mom asked why I wasn't coming home, and I told her I wanted to stay here to get to know the other girls. She said she understood, but I think she was a little hurt. I didn't tell her I have a date tonight. I suppose I could have had Chris pick me up at home, but I don't want any guys meeting my mom and dad until they have to.

The afternoon is crawling by at a snail's pace—no, make that like a snail stuck in the mud …going uphill…with a broken leg. That's how slow the afternoon is going. Maybe even slower.

I've done everything I can think of to pass the time. My homework for the week is done. I've played my guitar until my fingers hurt. I texted back and forth with Marissa, but then she had to go. So now I'm channel surfing the television, but there's nothing on except sports. If I was a guy, I'd be in heaven. But I'm not a guy, and I'm definitely not in heaven!

I come across "The Notebook" on TNT. Now I am in heaven. I love this movie! Allie and Noah are dancing in the street in the middle of the night—one of my all-time favorite scenes. Ohhh, to be Allie and to find a Noah. Have I mentioned I'm a sap for romance? No movie has done love and romance better than this one. I'm glued to my seat for an hour, and when the movie finally draws to a close, I've got a pile of wet tissues on the floor next to my chair. Like I said, I'm such a sap.

I wipe my eyes one last time and check the time. Four o'clock. Three hours until Chris picks me up. Now what?

I check the channel guide, hoping TNT will be repeating the movie, the way they sometimes do, so I can watch it from the beginning. But they're not. The next movie isn't even a love story—it's something with cyborgs and zombies. Iccck! Talk about a crummy programming decision. All the guys are already watching football—why put on a zombie movie? Give us girls something to watch, please!

I click through the channels one more time, but there's nothing remotely interesting to me. No love stories, no country music videos, no cool crossover shows like that one with Taylor Swift and Def Leopard. I sigh and switch off the TV.

I should have gone to the campus bookstore this morning and bought *Dracula*. Then I'd have something to read, at least. I could still go get it, but by the time I walked there and back, it would be time to start getting ready.

Thinking about getting ready is beginning to make me nervous. I've got my hopes up for tonight, but that only makes me more nervous. Aim small, girl, I tell myself. Be the cautious girl you've always been. Small expectations mean small disappointments. I've learned that lesson well.

Still, there are decisions to make. How should I do my hair? What should I wear? I'm such a dork about these things.

I go stand in front of the mirror. I wish Marissa was here. Why did her sister's birthday have to be this weekend? It's so not fair. She told me I should wear my new boots and new shirt with my leggings. Something about making sure I "seal the deal." Seal the deal? What am I, trying to sell a car or something? Is that outfit even appropriate for a first date?

I stretch out on my bed and try to relax, wishing I had more experience with this dating stuff. How did I manage to go my whole senior year without going on even one date? The answer pops immediately into my head and brings a feeling of sadness with it. It was because of Justin, of course. Not that I blame him. No, I blame only myself. But he was the reason, for sure. I close my eyes and remember....

*It's a cool Sunday afternoon in the middle of November. Justin and I are sitting on an old fallen log in a park not far from my house. He looks great, as usual. He's wearing his favorite jeans and a light green hoodie that makes his green eyes pop. We've been talking and laughing for over an hour. Nobody makes me feel as good as Justin does.*

*I've been in love with him ever since we met in*

*English class in the second half of junior year. He's everything I could ever ask for in a guy—smart, cute, honest and open. He's unpretentious, too. I don't even care that he's one of the best players on the basketball team.*

*I know he likes me, too. We talk all the time, and text almost every night. There's just one tiny problem—Nicole!*

*Justin likes me, but he's in love with Nicole. They've been going out since junior year. Even I have to admit Nicole is hot, but she treats Justin like crap. He's always bitching and moaning about it to me. How she doesn't understand him, doesn't really listen to him, doesn't care about what he thinks.*

*That's what he's saying to me now. Telling me about an argument they had last night, and how Nicole just kept trashing everything he said.*

*I'd love to tell him I would never do that, but I don't, of course. If only I could pound some sense into his beautiful head. Tell him to look past Nicole's hot outfits and see her as a person. Tell him how shallow she is. How he deserves someone so much better. Someone like me.*

*Instead, I mumble something about how she'll get over it, like she always does. And now here comes that beautiful smile again.*

*"I'm glad you're my bud, Heather. You always know how to cheer me up."*

*Ugggh!* Bud. *I hate that word. But to him, that's what we are. Best buddies. He can't see past Nicole.*

And that's how things stayed my whole senior year. I spent the entire year thinking Justin would finally see the light and come to his senses, but he never did. I thought we belonged together, but he obviously didn't see it that way. Maybe he'll wake up one day years from now and realize what he missed. That won't do me any good, though.

I haven't seen him in a couple of months. He accepted a basketball scholarship out of state, and left at the beginning of the summer to go work out with the team or something. At least he finally dumped Nicole. She's here at State, but I don't know if she's living on campus. I wonder if I'll ever see Justin again.

Anyhow, so now here I am, all stressed out about a first date. Most girls probably get over this in high school, but I never let myself have the chance to get used to it. I'd like to blame Justin, but I know it's my fault. That doesn't make it any easier though.

I get up and start ruffling through my closet. It's going to take me a while to decide what to wear, so I may as well get started. I've got nothing better to do.

First decision: pants or a skirt. If I can decide on that, a top should be easy, I hope. Dresses are out—this is a casual date. Good thing, too, since I only have two dresses in my closet and I don't really like either one. Jeans would be easy, and comfortable—but I'm afraid mine are *too* casual. It's only a movie and pizza, but what if Chris dresses up a bit? Now, if I owned some designer jeans it might be different. But I don't, of course.

I eliminate jeans.

I pull out three skirts and two pairs of pants and lay them out on the bed. Ugggh! Who bought this stuff? It all looks so high schoolish. Maybe this is why Justin never saw me as more than a buddy. I don't want Chris to see me the same way. I'm definitely going to have to make another trip to The Buff with Marissa. She'll be all for that, but unfortunately, it doesn't do me any good right now.

Maybe my new silk shirt can save one of the skirts. I slip into a black one that stops just above my knees, then go back to the closet to get the shirt. I put it on and check myself out in the mirror.

No good. I like the shirt, but it's really too long for this skirt. I try tucking it in, but I don't like the way it looks. I try it with a longer navy skirt, but I don't like that look, either. I'm running out of options. I may have to go with the leggings and boots by default.

I put off a final decision. It's time to hop into the shower, anyway. My hair takes forever to dry, so unless I want to tuck it into a bun behind my head, I need to get going.

I look in the mirror again. This time, I'm liking what I see—kind of, at least. I'm wearing my hunting outfit. The combo is definitely both cooler and hotter than anything I've ever worn. And, I have to admit, the whole thing is really comfortable. Leggings and soft boots definitely rock the comfort factor. But do I have the guts to wear it outside of my room? The movie will be dark, of course, and for pizza we'll be sitting in a booth, so maybe it won't be too bad. And it's not like I have a lot of choices. Okay, hunting outfit it is, winner by default.

Now, what about my hair? Should I wear it down and loose, or pull it back? Down and loose, I can hide behind it if I need to. Pulled back, it'll be out of my way, one less thing to worry about. Decisions, decisions, decisions. I stress about it for a few minutes, then opt for comfort over concealment. Pulled back it is. I grab a scrunchy and gather my hair into a thick ponytail.

A soft knock sounds at my door. Oh my god! Is it seven o'clock already? I take one last look in the mirror. I see several things I want to change, but there's no time. That's probably a good thing, though. If I had any more time, I'm sure I'd drive myself crazy, if I'm not there already. Still, I make one final adjustment, flipping my hair forward over my left shoulder as I cross to the door. Now I can at least run my fingers through it if I get nervous. *If* I get nervous? Ha! My fingers are already dancing in my hair as I pull the door open.

Chris is standing there, smiling confidently. He looks great. He's wearing dark gray pants and a black button shirt with vertical gold stripes. The sleeves are rolled up to his elbows. He looks casual and classy at the same time. I wonder how long it took him to decide what to wear. Five minutes, probably, if that. I don't think guys stress over this stuff like girls do. Especially girls like me. I'm glad I decided against jeans.

I've barely opened the door when the smile drops from Chris's face. He stands there, staring at me with his mouth slightly open. His eyes travel slowly down from my face to my body. I feel like I'm on display, and that I'm failing the inspection. I knew I should have met him out in front of the dorm—I could have just jumped into his truck—but he wanted to be a gentleman and pick me up at my door. So now I'm stuck, standing here with nowhere to hide.

I look down at myself, wondering what he's seeing. A thousand thoughts race through my brain. Did I spill something on myself? Am I too skinny? Too fat? Does he hate my outfit?

*Say something, Chris, please. No, never mind, don't say anything. I don't want to know.* I wish I could just disappear, or teleport myself somewhere. Anywhere but where I'm standing right now.

I'm never going on another date. Never, ever!

## CHAPTER 9

"**Y**ou look amazing," Chris says finally. "Absolutely amazing."

The smile is back on his face. I notice his eyes keep straying down to my legs and my boots. A moment ago I wanted to disappear. Now I'm floating. I feel like I'm in heaven. Thank you, Marissa!

"Thanks," I manage to say. "You look pretty good yourself."

"I'd ask for a quick tour," he jokes, "but I can see the whole place from here."

"Very funny," I say. I take a quick glance over my shoulder. "It is pretty small, isn't it? But I'm *very* happy to be here, believe me. Besides, we can't all live in the Ritz."

The Ritz is the nickname given by students to Sedgewick Hall, where Chris lives. It's the newest dorm on campus, and it's got nothing but suites, with each student getting his own bedroom. All the furnishings are also new, of course. Since dorm choices are given by seniority, no way can a freshman get into the Ritz. Not that I'd want to spend the extra money, anyhow. And Sedgewick is way over on the edge of campus, much farther from most of the classrooms than my dorm.

"No, we can't," Chris says. He flashes his teasing grin. "But if you behave yourself, I just might give you a tour one of these days. No charge."

Uh, oh. Alarm bells begin to go off in my head. Is he *already* thinking about getting me back to his place? I am sooo not ready for that. My mind flashes ahead to the end of tonight's date, imagining a totally awkward scene. How do I decline his advances, with-out seeming like a scared fifteen-year-old? Or hurting his feelings? *Calm down girl*, I tell myself, *he's just making a joke. You're getting waaay ahead of yourself.*

I look at him more closely. Happily, I don't see any hint of a double meaning in his expression. Yeah, he's just making a joke... I hope. Sometimes, it's really difficult being me. My imagination is usually my own worst enemy—conjuring up disasters that never come to be. I remember something we learned in high school that Mark Twain said: "I'm an old man and have known a great many troubles, but most of them never happened." That's me, all right. I've endured a few real troubles, sure, but most existed simply in my mind. I wonder if I'll ever outgrow that. Right now, it doesn't seem like it.

Chris seems blissfully unaware of my inner turmoil. I am profoundly grateful for that. It's bad enough that I have to be inside my head. I certainly wouldn't wish it on him.

"Do you like living in Sedgewick?" I ask, changing the subject without really changing it.

"Yeah, I do. One of my roommates is kind of an a-hole, but the other two are cool. Whenever he gets to be too much to take, I just retreat to my room. Luckily, he spends a lot of time away from the dorm."

"Marissa and I get along great, so I don't have to worry about anything like that."

Chris glances at his watch. "You ready to go?" he asks. "The movie starts in twenty-five minutes. If we want to have time to get some popcorn, we'd better get going."

"Yep, I'm all set."

I pull the door closed and follow Chris across to the elevator. The door slides open almost as soon as he pushes the button. There's a girl inside I don't recognize, but she makes no move to come out. I guess she got in on the way up, even though she's going down. She gives Chris an approving look, but he barely glances at her. He certainly doesn't seem to have noticed the way she looked at him. I like that a lot.

Just to be safe, though, I edge closer against Chris, making sure this girl knows he's mine. Mine for tonight, anyhow, I remind myself.

The movie was great—funny and romantic, just the way I like. Chris and I are now sitting across from each other in a booth in the back corner of a popular pizza joint a block from campus. The red vinyl benches are worn and lumpy, but I don't care. The varnished wood tabletop bears the scratched markings of decades of young revelers. I see several hearts with initials carved inside—I wonder if my initials will ever appear inside a heart somewhere. With my track record, I'll probably have to carve them myself, along with a fake guy's initials.

The restaurant is jammed with students. I'm pretty sure many of them are over twenty-one, because it's pretty boisterous in here. It's hard to imagine this kind of volume without alcohol playing at least some part. Chris and I have to speak up to hear each other over the raucous chatter.

"The movie was really good," I say. "You made a great choice, Chris. Thanks."

"Well, I was pretty sure you wouldn't be into car chases and explosions," he says, "so that narrowed the choices a bit."

"Did you like it, too?" I ask.

"Yeah, I did. I thought it was pretty funny."

"I love Katherine Heigl," I say. "Her movies are always so funny, and they usually end happily."

I don't see the need to share that I like her so much because she's tall and usually gawky and awkward—like me—in her movies, but in the end she gets the guy and lives happily ever after.

A cute pony-tailed waitress bustles over to take our order. She's almost certainly a fellow State student. She smiles and asks what we want.

"Let's see if we can agree on a pizza as well as we did on the movie," Chris says. "What do you like?"

"Pepperoni," I say.

"Pepperoni is good," Chris says. "And how about some mushrooms, too?"

"Perfect. I love mushrooms."

"Pepperoni and mushrooms it is, then," he tells the waitress, who jots the order down on her pad and scurries away.

"That was pretty easy," Chris says.

"Were you worried I'd be one of those girls who'd

want nothing but veggies on her pizza?" I ask.

"Maybe a little," he admits. "Especially since you're so slender."

I'm glad he said "slender" instead of "skinny." Guys like slender. Skinny, not so much.

"What's a pizza without at least a little grease," I say, smiling.

Chris smiles back. "You'll get no argument from me on that."

We spend another ten minutes talking about the movie, laughing together at some of the funnier parts, until our waitress returns and places our pizza on the table between us. It smells delicious, and I can feel the heat radiating up onto my face.

"Enjoy your pizza," she says.

Maybe I'm imagining it, but her eyes seem to linger on Chris a moment more than necessary. She spins away and leaves before I can be sure. Chris gives no sign he noticed anything, so maybe I was imagining it. *Get a grip, girl!* First the girl in the elevator, and now the waitress. I'm becoming way too paranoid. And even if she did sneak a bit of a look, so what? Would I rather date someone no other girls want to look at?

Chris lifts a piece of pizza from the platter and deposits it onto my plate.

"Enjoy," he says as he grabs a piece for himself.

I take a small, careful bite. It's really hot, and despite my caution, I burn the roof of my mouth a bit. The pizza is deliciously greasy, though. Just the way I like it. Well worth a little pain.

"Mmmmm, it's really good," I say.

"Sure is," Chris agrees.

His eyes fasten on mine. His eyes are gorgeous, but I'd rather look at them when he's not looking directly back into mine. I look down at the slice of pizza in my hands instead and prepare to take another bite.

"Tastes almost as good as you look," he adds.

The pizza stops halfway to my mouth. I can feel myself blushing. I glance up at Chris for a moment, but then shift my gaze from his face and stare into the flickering red glass candle jar on the table. How do I respond to a statement like that? Part of me is really happy he likes the way I look, but a bigger part of me is uncomfortable with the flattery. I don't even know if he's being serious or just joking around. I hope it's a little of both. I wish I was one of those girls who could reply to something like that with a simple "thanks." Life would be sooo much easier.

I put the pizza down and lean back against the cushioned booth. Chris is looking at me expectantly, a half-smile on his face. I guess I have to respond somehow, but I have no idea what to say.

An idea pops into my head. What the heck, I think. It worked once.

"Red, blue, green, black," I say.

Chris bursts out laughing, so loudly that the couple at the table next to us both turn and look at him. He puts his napkin over his mouth and waves an apology to them.

"Good one," he says to me when he brings his laughter under control. "Touché."

He shakes his head, still grinning, and then returns to his pizza. I happily take another bite of mine. Yum! I hope

I look *half* as good as it tastes….

We're standing outside my dorm. Our first date is drawing to a close.

It's a beautiful night. Above us, a fingernail moon floats high in a sky pinpricked by a flickering canopy of stars. The soft, rhythmic chirping of an invisible army of crickets buzzes all around us, and I can hear "Our Song" by Taylor Swift playing softly from somewhere in the dorm. How fitting. The couple in the song had the sound of a slamming screen door as their song—I guess Chris and my song will be the music of the crickets. I kind of like that. Much better than a slamming door, for sure.

The air is warm and slightly moist on my cheek, like a chaste kiss. I've been pretty relaxed most of the night—relaxed for me, at least—but I'm beginning to feel nervous again. What do I say if he asks to come up? Or if he tries to kiss me? And what if he doesn't try to kiss me? That might be even worse! My fingers begin stroking through my hair.

I sense that Chris is a tiny bit nervous, too, which makes me feel a little better.

"I had a great time tonight," he says.

"Me, too."

I did have a really good time, and I was pretty sure Chris enjoyed himself as much as I did, but it's nice to hear it confirmed. "It was really fun," I add.

"Does that mean you'll say yes if I ask you out again?"

*Of course I would!* I scream inside my head. But that's not a cautious girl reply. And what's with that question, anyhow? It's not like Chris to be so indirect. I guess I was right—he *is* a little nervous. I decide to be indirect, too.

"I might," I say, smiling. "I guess you'll just have to wait and see."

He grins. "I hate waiting. Would you like to go out Friday night?"

I force myself to wait a second or two. I don't want to appear *too* anxious.

"Yes, I'd like that."

"Great. It's a date, then."

He leans forward. Oh my god, I think he's going to kiss me. What do I do now?

I turn my head slightly, offering him my cheek, but at the same time, he twists his head sideways, aiming for my cheek. But my cheek isn't there anymore. My mouth is.

Our lips meet, for a brief instant, because he was just going for a quick peck on the cheek. Still, his lips feel wonderful.

He pulls back, laughing. "Well, that was awk-ward," he says.

"Yeah, it was," I say. I want to add "but nice," but I don't dare.

"I'll call you about Friday," he says. He puts his hands on my shoulders. "Don't move this time."

He leans forward and kisses me on the cheek, letting his lips linger there for a moment. It's not really possible that his lips are burning my skin, is it?

"That's better," he says. "Good night, Heather."

I turn and go inside, smiling. That was a pretty perfect ending to a pretty perfect night.

## CHAPTER 10

**I**'m pacing back and forth in my room, too wound up to go to bed, too wound up even to sit down. I keep replaying our date in my head. It's ecstasy and it's agony. Ecstasy from remembering how Chris's eyes sparkled, how easy it was to talk to him, how much we laughed. We had so much fun. So why can't I just stop there, replaying all the fun? No, not me. I have to visit the dark side, agonizing over everything he said, everything he did, trying to figure out what it meant, wondering if he really likes me as much as I think he does. As much as I hope he does. Sure, he asked me out again, but maybe that's just less awkward than saying goodnight without any mention of a second date. I just don't know—I've got so little experience with first dates.

Some lines from Taylor Swift's "Am I Ready for Love" pop into my head. I wonder if I'm ready for everything that goes with being in love—the joy, the pain, the wondering. She even calls it a game—and I'm terrible at games. Ugh…I'm not ready for anything!

I think back to how our date ended, with a kiss on the cheek. Is that good? Or bad? Did it mean Chris didn't want to move too fast, that he sensed I was nervous and he was being considerate? That would be awesome. Or did it mean he didn't feel romantic with me? Maybe he doesn't find me sexy. Maybe those leggings and boots make my legs look too skinny. Maybe it was just a "let's be friends" kiss? God, I hope not. I am so not going down that road again, doing the best buddies thing. I have to think I learned something from my time with Justin.

I'd love to distract myself with my guitar, but it's after midnight, and the walls are thin. I checked next door, but the door was closed and no light showed under it. Stacie and Jill are either still out somewhere, or they're sleeping. Maybe if I play real softly, it would be okay.

Who am I kidding? I'm too jacked up to play softly. So no guitar. Now what? No way will I be able to sleep anytime soon.

I turn on the television, hoping to find distraction there. I flip aimlessly through the channels, finally settling on Saturday Night Live. It's pretty funny, and for the first time since I said goodnight to Chris, my mind focuses on something other than my date.

But the show ends much too soon, and I can't find anything else worth watching. I wonder if Marissa is still awake. Maybe I'll text her. My phone buzzes, as if it's read my mind. I bet it's Marissa, wanting the 411 on how my date went. Got an hour, girl?

I check the text. It's not from Marissa—it's from Chris! "Hey, RBGB…I really had fun 2night. Hope U did 2. ttys." What the heck is RBGB? It sounds like a connection port on my laptop or something. Suddenly, I get it, and I crack up. RBGB equals Red, Blue, Green, Black. Oh my god—he's too funny!

My brain finally slows down from overdrive. He wouldn't have texted if he wasn't interested in me. A peaceful smile stretches my lips. I think maybe I can go to sleep now. One last thing to do first, though.

"Ditto" I reply.

It's nearly ten o'clock when I finally drag myself out of bed. It took me a little while to fall asleep, but once I nodded off, I was out for the night. If I dreamed at all, I don't remember it. I check my phone, calling up last night's text, just to make sure THAT wasn't a dream. It wasn't. I smile again at the RBGB thing.

I go downstairs for a quick breakfast. There are eight or ten other girls there, but none that I know, so I wolf down a bowl of Cheerios over in the corner and head back up to my room.

I've got the whole day to myself. Marissa won't be back until later this afternoon. It's beautiful outside—warm and sunny. I think I'll go for a long walk. There's a big county park not too far from campus that's supposed to have lots of pretty trails. That should be fun—I haven't taken a real walk since I got to school last week. I think about texting Chris to see if he wants to join me. Yeah, right. Marissa might be able to do that, but no way I can, not at this point, anyhow. Besides, I don't want to seem too eager. Aren't girls supposed play a little hard to get? I wish dating came with a manual.

I slip into a pair of black exercise shorts and a white tank top and put on my Nikes. I think about taking my iPod, but most of my walk will be in the woods and I want to listen to the nature sounds. I grab a bottle of water and head out the door.

The park is less than a mile from campus, so in fifteen minutes I'm turning into the entrance. I skirt the edge of a gravel parking lot and a shaded picnic area dotted with wooden tables and metal barbecue grills. Beyond the picnic area is the park's central attraction, a large lake. Rowboats and paddleboats for rent are tied to a short pier on the near shore. A few boaters are already out on the lake, floating idly, some with fishing poles hanging over the side. I stop and watch for a moment, wondering what kind of fish they're catching. Or if they're catching anything at all. I've never done any fishing, but it sure looks peaceful and relaxing. I think actually catching something might ruin that, at least for me.

I continue with my walk. Over on a large grass field to my left, a group of shirtless young men are playing soccer. I bet Chris looks good without his shirt. The thought makes me blush, even though there's no one near me. *Down, girl*, I tell myself. *Take it easy*.

Other than the soccer players and boaters, I see only a few other people in the park. A man and woman about the same age as my parents are sitting in folding chairs near one of the grills. Thin white smoke wafts up from the grill, and the succulent smell of slow-roasting meat makes my mouth water. From the amount of supplies covering three of the picnic tables, I'm thinking the couple is making preparations for a fairly big gathering.

The park's relative emptiness doesn't surprise me. It's still not even eleven o'clock yet. I'll bet by lunchtime the place will be much more crowded, with the day as beautiful as it is. Lots of people probably slept in today, or are still sitting in church.

Up ahead, several trails lead up into the woods, just as the park's web page promised. There's one that circles the lake along the top of the ridge, and that's the one I mean to try this morning. A carved sign on a wooden post guides me to the path I want. A second sign at the trailhead informs hikers that it's a three-mile loop. Counting the walk to and from the park, that will make about five miles—just about perfect. I forge ahead. This is going to be fun.

The trail is wide enough for three people to walk abreast, and the dirt surface is packed hard, making walking easy. It slopes upward into the trees, but not steeply enough to slow me down. The woods are beautiful—lush with end of summer growth. Young saplings and leafy underbrush flank the path, while just a bit farther from the trail majestic oak and ash trees spread a green canopy that blocks out all but the tiniest pieces of blue sky. I see lots of gnarled dogwood trees, too. The blossoms are long gone, replaced by shiny red berries. The berries look like they could be tasty, but I know they're poisonous. A few berries won't kill you, but they could make you awfully sick. I think there might be a broken heart song in there somewhere—comparing love to poison berries or something. It's too bad I don't write music. Not really, though. I'm much too happy to write a broken heart song.

The air feels at least five degrees cooler in the shade of the trees. A gentle breeze rustles the leaves, and birds are whistling cheerfully to one another from the higher branches. I wish I knew what they were saying.

Something rustles through the bushes off to my left. Probably just a squirrel or a rabbit. But it could be a deer, so I stop for a moment, my eyes trying to pierce the undergrowth to see what it is. The leaves are too thick, though, and whatever it was makes its escape unseen.

I resume my walk, climbing steadily for almost a mile. The trail is steeper now. I catch a few glimpses of the lake below me to the right, but for the most part my view is blocked by the trees. Finally, I reach the top of the ridge. There's a break in the trees here, and I have an unobstructed view down to the lake. It's breathtaking. The bright blue sky reflects off the water, giving it a beautiful blue hue, and gentle ripples stirred by the breeze sparkle gold in the sunlight. There are already more boats on the water than when I began my walk.

I've worked up a good sweat and I'm breathing heavily from the climb, so I stop to take a long swallow of water and to admire the view. It doesn't get much better than this. I spend about ten minutes enjoying the beauty and the peaceful quiet before continuing my hike. The trail follows the top of the ridge for nearly a mile, so I get lots more views of the lake before the path finally turns back down the hill. All downhill from here, I tell myself.

As I guessed, the picnic area is much more crowded than when I passed by less than an hour ago. The smells of cooking food are stronger and more varied now, and my stomach begins to rumble with hunger. I guess a bowl of cereal isn't quite enough to fuel such a good workout, despite what the commercials tell us. Maybe if I make myself look hungry enough, someone will invite me to join them for lunch!

Alas, I make it past all the tables and grills without a single invite. When I get back to the dorm I'm definitely heading straight to the cafeteria. As I exit the park, I realize I haven't thought about Chris for almost an hour—since the shirtless thing. Hooray for me!

## CHAPTER 11

I step out of the elevator and see my door is part way open. Marissa must have gotten back earlier than she expected. I can't wait to tell her about my date.

"Hey, Marissa," I call as I hurry into the room. Before I can say anything else, I realize Marissa is not alone. Two girls I don't know are also here. "Oops. Sorry. I didn't know you had company."

Marissa is sitting on her bed, legs stretched out in front of her, her back against the wall, an open can of Red Bull in her hand. She's wearing a black T-shirt and teal leggings. The shirt has a game of Tic-tac-toe painted in gold on the front. Instead of X's and O's, it has X's and hearts. The hearts have won the game, filling a diagonal row from bottom left to top right. When I pull my eyes away from the game on her chest, I see that her fingernails and toenails are painted to match her leggings. No way could I ever see myself with teal nails.

"No problem," Marissa says. "This is Beth and Katie, from down the hall. We were just hangin' out."

I try to mask my disappointment at not finding Marissa alone as I exchange hellos with the two girls.

Katie is very pretty, with long black hair almost to her waist and a dark tan. A royal blue cami paired with white capri pants shows off her tan. She's sitting in the lotus position on the rug in the center of the floor, looking completely comfortable. I wish my legs would bend like that.

Beth is sitting on Marissa's desk chair. She's tall, though not as tall as me, and much thicker, with shoulder-length hair brown hair. She's wearing jeans and a tight gray T-shirt stretched across full breasts. Big pink letters on the shirt proclaim I'VE BEEN NAUGHTY. Probably not the shy type, I decide.

"So, what gives?" Marissa asks after we all finish saying hello. "You came rushing in here like you'd just won backstage passes to a Taylor Swift concert or something."

I sit down on my bed and draw my knees up against my chest. I don't really want to talk about my date in front of two girls I just met.

"Oh, nothing really. It can wait."

"C'mon, Heather," Marissa says. "Beth and Katie are cool. Give it up."

Now what do I do? I can feel my mouth going dry. I am so not good at this social stuff. I'm in college now, I remind myself. Time to grow up. Or try to, at least. I take a deep breath and decide to go for it.

"I wanted to tell you about my date with Chris," I say.

"Sweet!" Marissa says. "Time for some Girl Council."

"First date?" Katie asks.

"Yeah," I say. I decide not to add it was my first date

in a very long time.

"Great," Beth says. "Tell us all about it." She grins. "And make sure you don't leave out any of the juicy details."

Oh god, now what? They're probably expecting something all hot and heavy, and all I've got is a g-rated story. I'm going to sound like a high school girl, I know it. A very young and naive high school girl.

Marissa must know how I'm feeling, because she jumps in to rescue me.

"Down, girls," she says. "Heather's a bit shy. Don't expect anything too hot and heavy." She turns to me. "Why don't you break the ice by telling Katie and Beth how you and Chris met. They'll get a kick out of that."

So that's just what I do. I tell them how Marissa shoved me at Chris and about the red, blue, green, black thing. By the time I finish, we're all laughing and I'm feeling much better.

"That's hilarious," Beth says. "Really hilarious."

"Hilarious, *and* it worked," Katie says, chuckling. "That makes it even cooler."

"Did you wear your new outfit last night?" Marissa asks me.

"Yeah, I did."

"What was the outfit?" Katie asks.

"Boots, black leggings and a grey silk shirt," Marissa explains.

"Nice," Beth says. "With those long legs, you must have looked hot. Wait until he sees you in a pair of Daisy Dukes."

I don't bother to tell Beth I don't own anything even

close to Daisy Dukes.

"She does look hot, believe me," Marissa says. She turns to me. "Did Chris say anything about how you looked?"

"He said I looked amazing," I say. "I almost didn't wear it, but I couldn't find anything else I liked. We need to make another trip to The Buff."

"I love that place," Katie says. "They have so much cool stuff."

"Hey, is this guy on Facebook?" Beth asks. "I want to see what he looks like."

I can't believe I haven't thought of that. I'm such a dork. I just don't use Facebook very much, so it never crossed my mind to check out Chris's page. I grab my laptop and sit back down on my bed. The girls crowd around me.

"Fifteen friends?" Beth asks as my profile page loads onto the screen. "What are you, some kind of monk? I've got over four hundred."

"I told you she was shy," Marissa says. "She only had fourteen till she added me."

"Add me and Beth," Katie says. "We'll get your total up there in no time."

"You've got a notification," Beth says. "Maybe someone else wants to be your friend. Maybe it's Chris. Click it."

I click the little globe, and sure enough, up pops a friend request from Chris. A warm feeling spreads through me.

"Should I accept?" I ask innocently.

Marissa shoves me playfully on the shoulder. "Ha,

ha," she says. "Very funny."

I laugh and click "accept."

"Sixteen friends now," Marissa says, smiling. "The sky's the limit."

"Okay, now go to his profile," Beth says. "Let us check him out."

"He's cute," Katie says when his picture appears.

"And it doesn't say he's in a relationship," Beth adds. "That's always good to see. Click the picture. I want to see a close-up."

"Wow, nice eyes," Katie says when the larger pic fills the page.

I click on another couple of his pictures and we all agree he's a keeper. I log off and shut down my computer. Marissa stays seated on the bed next to me, while Katie and Beth return to the chairs.

"So, did you two do the movie and pizza thing last night?" Marissa asks.

"Yeah." I tell them about the movie and how much fun we had at the pizza place. I save Chris's "as good as it tastes" comment for when I'm alone with Marissa.

"Okay, get to the good stuff, Heather," Beth says. "Good-night kiss? More? Spill it."

My cheeks begin to grow warm. I don't really want to talk about this, but they're all staring at me expectantly. I know this is the kind of stuff girls love to talk about, but I've haven't done it since Brian and Gaby. And that seems like a lifetime ago.

"There's not all that much to say," I tell them. "It was kind of awkward."

Marissa grins. "Now why doesn't that surprise me?"

"What happened?" Katie asks. "What was awkward?"

"He walked me to the door of the dorm. I was pretty nervous. I'm sure he could tell, so he just went to kiss me on the cheek."

"That's it?" Beth asks, clearly disappointed by the lack of anything juicy. "Just a kiss on the cheek?"

"Well, not quite." I'm feeling really stupid now, but I guess I have to finish my story. I hope they'll think it's funny, not pathetic.

"I'm not really sure how it happened," I say, "but when he went to kiss me, I turned my head. I didn't know he was already planning to kiss my cheek. Somehow, we both turned our heads just right and he ended up kissing me on the lips. We were both so surprised, it didn't last long." I smile. "But I liked it."

"What's not to like?" Beth says, grinning.

I want to talk more about the kiss, but it's another thing I think I'll hold off on until I'm alone with Marissa. I look over at her and find her looking closely at me.

"What is it?" she asks.

"Huh?"

"You've got something on your mind you're not saying," she says. "I can tell. What is it?"

Once again, all three of them are staring at me. My heart starts hammering in my chest. I guess I'm not going to get to wait.

"I, uh, wanted to ask you something," I say. "About the kiss."

"What about it?"

This is one of the things I've been worrying over the most. I really wish I was alone with Marissa, but maybe it will be good to get more than one opinion. I plunge on.

"Do you think it's bad that he just wanted to kiss me on the cheek? I mean, if he really liked me, wouldn't he have tried for more?"

"Maybe," Marissa says. "But maybe not."

"Most guys would," Beth says. "But most guys are jerks. Maybe Chris is one of the rare ones—a nice guy."

"If he is," Katie says, smiling, "see if he has a brother."

We all laugh.

"Didn't you say you thought Chris could tell how nervous you were?" Marissa asks.

"Yeah, I think so. I mean, how could he not?"

"So maybe he just didn't want to make you feel any more uncomfortable," Katie says. "If he tries for more of a kiss and you're not ready, things can get awkward real fast, trust me."

"Did he say he wanted to see you again?" Marissa asks.

"Yeah, he did." I decide not to repeat how we danced around that topic. "For Friday night."

"Then there's your answer," Marissa says. "He likes you. Case closed."

"Unless he figured asking you out again was the easiest way for him to escape," Beth says teasingly.

"Stop it, Beth," Marissa says. "You'll give Heather an ulcer." She turns back to me. "He friended you on Facebook, he asked you for a second date, and he texted you after he got home. He likes you. Period."

I sure hope so, because I really like him….

# CHAPTER 12

I arrive twenty minutes early for my vampire lit class. Not because it's a long walk from my dorm—which it isn't—and not because I'm obsessively punctual—which I am. I'm here early to keep myself out of a potentially awkward situation.

I want to make sure I get here before Chris, so I don't have to make any decision about whether to sit next to him or not. I know it's probably not that big a deal—Girl Council has all agreed that he likes me—but it makes me nervous thinking about it. What if he *doesn't* want to sit next to me for some reason? Better that it's *his* decision, not mine. I keep telling myself to stop all the negative thinking, but a lifetime of thinking that way isn't easy to give up.

Anyhow, the room is almost empty. Only about a half-dozen kids are here this early, so I have my choice of seats. I decide to make it easy for Chris to find me, so I head down the second to last aisle and take the same seat as last week. Now it's up to him—if he wants to sit with me, great. He can come join me. I sure hope he does, or I'm going to feel rejected. And I'm not sure how I would handle that.

I wonder if all girls are this paranoid about this dating stuff. Somehow, I doubt it.

The minutes crawl by. This is the downside to getting here so early—too much time to think. I pull my hair out of its ponytail and let it fall loose over my shoulders, giving myself something to play with. I wonder what the other kids would think if they knew I changed my clothes three times before coming here, trying to figure out the right thing to wear. I want to look good, but I have to remember that it's just class, not a date. Marissa and I haven't gone back to The Buff yet, so I had only my old stuff to choose from. I finally settled on what I probably would have worn if there were no Chris—my ripped jeans and one of my nicer T-shirts, a brown Hollister one. So I'm comfortable and at least mildly stylish.

The room slowly begins to fill, mostly with kids coming in by themselves, but some arrive in pairs or even small groups. The back of the room seems to be more popular than the front, and the empty seats around me are vanishing rapidly. I keep looking over my shoulder to the door, but there's still no sign of Chris. I wonder if I should save the seat next to me. Then, if it's really crowded when he arrives, he'll have a good excuse to sit with me. Not that I want him to need an excuse, of course, and he probably doesn't stress about this stuff like I do anyway. Still, if it were me, I'd love for the only empty spot in the whole room to be next to him. I fold down the seat to my right and put my notebook on it.

About two minutes before class is going to start, Chris walks through the door. He's wearing a tight black

T-shirt and jeans. He looks good. The shirt has a braided collar with one open button and some kind of gold emblem over the heart, but I can't see what it is from here. He stops just inside the doorway and begins surveying the room. Looking for me, I hope. Should I wave to get his attention? Or would that be that too forward? Maybe I should just wait for us to make eye contact. Or maybe I should act like I'm not even looking for him. I'm debating whether to turn away or not when his eyes find mine and he smiles. Have I mentioned that I love his smile?

I smile back, and he heads toward my row. While he picks his way past all the kids between us, I grab my notebook from the seat beside me. No need to let him know I was saving it for him. Let him think he just got lucky. Maybe next time he'll get here a little earlier, and we'll have a chance to talk a bit before class.

"Hi, Heather," he says as he settles down onto the seat. "Were you saving this for me?"

How do I answer that? If I say yes, it'll show I'm interested, but he might think I'm desperate or needy or something. If I say no, he might think I don't like him that much, and I don't want that. God, dating is hard!

I decide to answer with a tease. Humor is a good way to say something without having to commit yourself to actually meaning it.

"Yeah," I say with a smile. "I've been saving it just for you... or any other tall good-looking guy who happened to want it."

He laughs. "In this class, I don't think I have too much to worry about. I doubt there are even ten guys in here. But I may have to spy on you in your other classes, to see what kind of action you're getting."

Am I sick that I kind of like the idea of him spying on me? Next thing you know, I'll be hoping he's a stalker.

"You look good," he says. "I like your hair loose like that."

I start to wonder if that means he didn't like it tied back, but for once I'm able to cut off my stressful thinking. He said I look good—let's leave it at that. Note to self, though—no more ponytails!

"Thanks," I say, as Professor Simpson appears on stage, saving me from having to say anything else.

Class flies by. Dr Simpson is a very entertaining speaker, and he asks some good questions. There are a couple of girls in class who seem to be vampire fanatics. One of them even looks like a vampire, with pale skin and dressed completely in black. Just a goth, though. The vampire fans provide some interesting back and forth with the professor. I neither ask nor answer any questions, nor does Chris. We exchange a few whispered comments during class, but for the most part, I try to keep my attention focused on the professor. Try, I said—I'm not always successful. A couple of times I steal a glance at Chris and see a bemused expression on his face. I don't think he takes this class too seriously. Like he said, it's an easy credit. Twice, I catch him looking at me. He doesn't turn away when I catch him, he just smiles at me. I fantasize about sitting here in class holding hands with him. How cool would that be?

Professor Simpson draws the class to a close by giving us our reading assignments. Reading about vampires is homework I can definitely handle, even though we're still on *Dracula*.

"Can I walk you home?" Chris asks.

*You'd better*, I say to myself. Out loud I say "that'd be great."

I wonder if he'll offer to carry my books. I only have my spiral notebook and a paperback copy of *Dracula*, and he doesn't seem to see the need to offer. I don't mind at all, though. He already scored points when he carried my shopping bag home from The Buff.

The walk back to the dorm is fun. Our conversation is easy and casual—nothing at all to make my paranoid brain kick in with worries or questions, which is definitely saying something. By the time we reach my dorm, I'm feeling comfortable and even a little bold.

"Do you want to come up for a little while," I ask. "You can meet Marissa."

"Sure," he says. "That'd be nice."

He pulls the door open and stands aside to let me past. *Bing!* More gentleman points for the boy. He also lets me enter the elevator first.

The door to my room is open. Katie and Marissa are inside, sitting on Marissa's bed and thumbing through a People magazine. I wonder where Beth is. She's going to hate missing out on the chance to check out Chris in person. The girls look up as we enter. Marissa closes the magazine immediately.

"Hi, guys," I say. "This is Chris. Chris, this is my roommate Marissa, and Katie, from down the hall."

Chris flashes a friendly smile. "Hi," he says. "Nice to meet you both. I've heard a lot about you, Marissa."

"Heather's mentioned you once or twice, too,"

Marissa replies with a grin. "At least, I think you're the guy she keeps talking about."

Oh great, just what I need. I feel myself beginning to blush. Maybe it wasn't such a great idea to invite Chris up.

"I hear I have you to thank for me meeting Heather," Chris says. "She claims you pushed her, but I think she was just making up an excuse to hit on me."

Marissa and Katie laugh. I blush more.

"Well, maybe I did give her a tiny little shove," Marissa says. "Just to get her past her shyness."

"Grab a chair, Chris," I say, changing the subject. I motion to the one in front of my desk.

He pulls the chair out and straddles it, with the back between his legs. He looks pretty comfortable and at home, not nervous at all. I imagine how I would be, meeting his roommates for the first time. A total wreck, I'm sure.

I sit on my bed with my back against the wall. I try to think of something to get a conversation going about something other than me and my shyness, but my mind is a blank. Luckily, Katie comes to the rescue.

"So, how is that vampire lit class, anyhow?" she asks Chris. "Seems like a strange class for a college to be offering."

"It's filled with lots of very scholarly information," Chris says, grinning.

"Yeah, I bet," Katie says, returning his grin.

And just like that, the conversation is off and running. Before long, we're all talking and laughing like friends who have known each other for years.

## CHAPTER 13

Two weeks fly by. College is way better than I expected, or even hoped. Algebra is hard and boring—a bad combination—but the rest of my classes are good. Psychology is really fun and interesting, and I get to sit with Chris in vampire class, so what could be better than that? The homework for all my courses is pretty manageable, and the reading for vampire lit is definitely fun. We've finished with *Dracula* and are now working on *Interview with the Vampire*. I'm about halfway through it. Parts of it are *very* sensual, and it's awakening feelings in me I didn't know I had.

Marissa and I are getting along great. We've become best friends already, and I feel like she's the older sister I never had, even though she's barely two months older than me. She just knows so much more about everything. We talk for at least a little while every night, and she's definitely helping me come out of my shell. But she's doing it nice and slowly, which is how I like it. And we made another trip to The Buff, so now I have some more cute stuff to wear. She talked me into getting a pair of denim Daisy Dukes—thanks a lot, Beth, for putting the idea in her head! She's dying to see me wear them with my leggings, but I told her maybe I'll be ready come next spring. Everything in its time.

We hang out with Katie and Beth a bunch, too, which has been fun, and we've become friendly with several other girls on our floor as well. I'm up to twenty-six Facebook friends now. Not many compared to all the other girls, I know, but almost twice as many as I had when I got here. I'm sure you're not surprised to hear I'm pretty careful about who I friend. And that my profile is restricted to friends.

Marissa, Katie and I have gone hiking twice in the county park, and we had lots of fun both times. Katie is going to be a biology major, and she knows tons about the plants and animals. I'm learning so much stuff, maybe I should ask the school for a credit for our hikes. Beth is invited, of course, but she always declines, saying she "doesn't do woods." Her loss.

I went home last Sunday afternoon for dinner. It was good to see my mom and dad, but it didn't take long—twenty minutes, maybe—before they started bickering and I remembered why I was so determined to live on campus in the first place. I didn't have my guitar to retreat to, and with no car, I was trapped there for almost four long, long hours. Finally, I pleaded homework and asked dad to drive me back to school. I was never so happy to see my math homework.

And then there's Chris. He's been great. We've had three dates, and I see him every week at vampire class. He walks me home after class, and sometimes comes up to hang with me and Marissa for awhile. He seems to really get me, because he's taking things nice and slow, and I'm very grateful for that. I think he can sense I'm a flight risk. My paranoid thinking is become rarer and rarer, though, which is definitely nice. I hope he doesn't go *too* slowly, though—we haven't had our first real kiss yet. I'm definitely ready. I think. At least I am every time I read some hot part of *Interview with the Vampire*. If Chris doesn't make a move soon, my "maybe he doesn't like me enough" thinking is liable to come back.

Maybe he'll do it tonight. He's taking me to a place on campus called The Joint where they have open mic night on Fridays. Kids get up and sing or tell jokes. Chris says it's pretty funny sometimes, and that some of the kids are pretty talented. He still doesn't know I play guitar. Nobody but Marissa does. She's good at keeping secrets, which is a really nice quality in a best friend. I've played for her a couple of times now, and she keeps telling me I'm really good. I'm still not ready to play for anyone else, though. Not even Katie and Beth. How these other kids are able to get up in front of a bunch of strangers and sing I'll never know.

Marissa and I are trying to figure out what I should wear to open mic night. Chris says it's really casual and I should wear something funky—like I even know what that means.

"I told you we should have bought you something with skulls on it," Marissa says, grinning. "When you want something a bit 'out there' you can never go wrong with skulls. Too bad none of my stuff will fit you."

"Yeah, because I've been just lusting after that skulls and hearts shirt of yours," I reply sarcastically, but with a smile. "No skulls for this girl, thank you."

But it actually is too bad Marissa and I are so different in size. She has a couple of things I think would be perfect. I wish I knew I was going to need something "funky" when we made our second trip to The Buff.

"We'll just have to get creative," Marissa says. "Mix and mismatch a little. But not too much. We want you looking good. It's a date, after all."

She starts fingering through my closet again, but then stops abruptly.

"Hey, wait a minute," she says excitedly. "I do have something I think you can use."

She races to her dresser and pulls open the bottom drawer. She starts rummaging through it, tossing stuff haphazardly onto the floor until she finds what she's looking for.

"Here it is."

She holds up a band of black cloth about six inches wide. I have no idea what it is. It looks like an oversized headband. She puts her hands inside it and pulls them apart. The material stretches.

"One size fits all," she says. "Well, maybe not all, but it'll fit you fine."

*Fit me fine?* What is she talking about? I have no idea how I'm supposed to wear that thing. It's not really a headband, that much I know. And no way am I wearing it like a tube top. And if she's thinking mini-skirt, she must be on drugs.

Marissa bursts out laughing. "You should see the look on your face, Heather. I can just imagine what's going through your head. Don't worry. It's an accessory, not a top or a bottom."

I breathe a sigh of relief. I'm still not sure how I'm supposed to wear it, but it seems a lot safer now.

"Go get that sweater we bought," Marissa says.

I pull the ivory cable knit sweater I got on my first trip to The Buff out of my dresser and slip it on over my head. It's pretty light, so I think it will be comfortable inside The Joint.

Marissa hands me the black band. "Now put this on over it, like a belt, right above your hips."

I stare down at the band for a moment, trying to decide if I should step into it or pull it on over my head. It doesn't really matter, I guess, so I step into it and pull it up around my waist. Marissa reaches over and adjusts it a bit, then pulls the hem of my sweater down so it's not baggy above the band.

"Perfect," she says. "Take a look."

I step over in front of the mirror. It *does* look good. The tight band accentuates what little difference I have between my waist and hips—almost like I have a real shape!

"I like it," I say.

"You can wear it with those jeans, but if you want to be a little bolder, put on your black leggings."

I spin around once in front of the mirror. I think this look is already bold enough for me.

"I think I'll stick with the jeans," I say.

Marissa grins. "Yeah, I figured you'd say that. At least wear your boots. They'll give your look a little more of an edge."

I put on my gray suede boots and decide I can handle

that much of an "edge." Now that the problem of what to wear is out of the way, I start putting on my makeup.

Chris arrives right on time, at seven o'clock. His punctuality is just another thing I like about him. His outfit is a total surprise. He's wearing a tight black T-shirt with a big gray screaming skull on the front—Marissa is already giving me an "I told you so" look—and black jeans. But it's what he's wearing on his head and on his feet that really catches my attention. He's sporting a cloth fedora hat, the kind Justin Timberlake and Jason Mraz often wear. The pale pink and dark brown plaid pattern is an eye-catcher, but the hat is sedate compared to his shoes—bright pink and white checkered canvas sneakers.

The outfit screams "geek," but it actually looks good on him. The hat makes him much taller than me, which I really like. I could even wear heels if I wanted—if I owned any, and wasn't afraid I'd fall off them. The tight shirt and jeans fit his slender form perfectly. A slightly less bright pair of sneaks would be more to my taste, though.

"Wow. You weren't kidding when you said dress funky," I say, smiling.

He does a quick pirouette. "You like?"

"Surprisingly, yeah," I say. "If you'd told me on the phone you'd be wearing this, I'd probably have said 'oh, no'." I look down at his feet. "Those sneaks are a bit much, though."

"I know," he says. "That's why I got 'em. Gotta look extra sharp in case I decide to get up on stage."

*Get up on stage?* What is he talking about? He never said anything about getting up on stage. I thought we were going just to watch.

"You're going to perform?"

"You never know," he says.

Well *I* know. No way in hell is this girl getting up on stage. No way, no how.

"What do you do?" I ask. "Sing? Tell jokes?"

"Nothing so boring," he says. "I recite poetry."

He's got to be kidding. I've never been to the place, but I'm pretty sure the crowd will kill him if he tries to recite poetry.

"Please tell me you're kidding," I say. I definitely don't want to be known as the girl with the guy who told poems.

"What, you don't like poetry?" He's grinning, so I'm pretty sure he's playing me.

"I think I'll start with this," he says. His voice turns deep and dramatic. "One…fishhh…twooo…fishhh……red fishhh…."

I roll my eyes. Yep, he's playing me. Marissa is laughing.

"That'll knock 'em dead, for sure," I say. "Seriously, though. What do you do?"

He smiles. "You'll have to wait and see."

I decide it's time to give him a little poke back. "Okay, but just so you know, if you bomb up there, doing whatever it is you do, I'm going to pretend I don't know you."

"Fair enough," he says, laughing. "By the way, you look great. Sexy, but a little edgy, too. Perfect for The Joint." He turns to Marissa. "Do I detect your hand in this outfit?"

Marissa grins. "Just a little," she says.

I pull the top of the black band an inch or so away from my waist with my thumbs. "This is hers," I say. "I hate to admit it, but I didn't even know what it was when she showed it to me. I had some pretty scary thoughts, though," I add with a smile.

Chris laughs. "I think I can imagine at least one of them. Might not be a bad idea."

"Bite your tongue," I tell him, laughing.

"We'd better get going," Chris says. "Open mic doesn't start 'til eight, but sometimes it gets crowded."

"I'm ready," I say. I turn to Marissa. "See you later."

"Have fun, kids," she says. She grins at me. "You behave yourself, Heather."

"Yes, Mom," I say. "I'll try."

"You sure you don't want to join us?" Chris asks her. "It's usually pretty fun."

"No thanks, I'm good," she replies. "It's nice to have a night off for a change."

Marissa isn't kidding. She has no problem finding dates—she just hasn't found a guy she's wanted to see more than once yet. A couple of the guys she's gone out with are still pestering her for second dates, but she says she can tell from one date whether a guy is a keeper or not. So far, I've been afraid to ask her what the qualifications are.

## CHAPTER 14

Outside, the sun is vanishing behind the deep green hills to the west of campus, leaving behind a blazing palette of pinks, golds, oranges and purples. It's literally breathtaking.

"Wow! How nice is that?" Chris says.

"It's beautiful," I say. "Just beautiful."

"Yes," Chris says. "Very beautiful."

I turn my head and see he's looking at me now, not the sky. Here comes the blushing again. I'm afraid to meet his eyes, so I look back at the sunset. I've never been very comfortable with flattery.

"It's so nice out, how about we walk to The Joint?" Chris asks.

It really is nice out. The air is pleasantly warm, with just the barest hint of a breeze. Birds are chirping their merry evening songs, and I can smell fresh cut grass from somewhere. The Joint is less than a mile from my dorm, so walking is a great idea.

"Yeah, let's walk. That'll be great."

Chris takes my hand, and we head down the street to the west, directly into the sunset. It's so gorgeous, it's almost like walking into a painting. Chris and I reached the hand holding stage over a week ago, but I still get a little thrill every time his fingers touch mine, especially when he gives me that quick squeeze he always does when our hands first touch. If this were a movie, this would be the closing shot—two young lovers strolling off into the sunset, hand in hand. Remember, I believe in fairy tales—I'm just really careful about letting myself think I'll ever be part of one. But who knows?

Walking with Chris like this is so awesome I wish The Joint were farther away, but we're there in less than twenty minutes. The bright colors of the sunset are now only a narrow band above the horizon, with the rest of the sky a mixture of dark grays and purples. The smell of hamburgers and grilled onions has replaced the fragrance of cut grass—still appealing, but in a less romantic way.

The Joint is a small, very casual restaurant that has operated on campus for decades. It's one of the few places to eat on campus not run by the college. It has no liquor license, but since most students aren't old enough to legally drink, that's not a problem. Besides, there are plenty of places for kids to drink illegally, if they want. The Joint serves a simple menu of hamburgers and hot dogs, as well as hot and cold sandwiches. Along with soft drinks, you can get energy drinks, several different coffees and fruit smoothies. Chris tells me that a few years ago, someone had the idea to host an open mic night, and the place has become more popular than ever.

There's no line outside, so after Chris pays the cover charge to a good-looking blond guy seated on a wooden stool next to the door, we're able to go right in.

We step through the double glass doorway into a single, nearly square room. It's not all that big, but it's crowded with tables. Even so, I doubt the place holds much more than a hundred people. It's about three-quarters full now. The smell of grilling beef is stronger here, reminding me I haven't eaten since lunch, and the chattering conversations are a bit louder than I would have expected. I'm guessing that at least some of the kids have had a few drinks before coming to watch the festivities.

I slide my arm inside the crook of Chris's elbow. "You take me to all the nicest places," I tease.

He laughs. "What, you don't like plain and crowded?" He leans over and kisses my hair. "It'll be fun, I promise. And the food is surprisingly decent."

The hostess guides us to a small round table on the far side of the room, closer to the back than the front, but as I said, the place isn't very big, so there really isn't a bad seat in the house. I take the chair facing the makeshift stage—a raised square platform no more than ten feet across covered with black felt—and Chris sits down opposite me. There's an old acoustic guitar leaning against the wall at the rear of the stage and a beat up piano to the right. I'm glad we're far enough from the front that no one will see which table Chris came from if he gets up onstage and bombs. The hostess hands us each a plastic menu and scurries away.

I look at around at the people near us. All college kids, of course. I spot a couple of fedoras, some pink and green streaked hair, and a bright green, blue and yellow plaid sports jacket the guy must be wearing as joke. He *has* to be a comedian. If not, I feel really sorry for the girl sitting next to him, who is actually kind of cute. I take that back—I feel sorry for her even if he is a comedian.

I flip open the menu. It's pretty basic. A few appetizers and four or five kinds of hamburgers with corny names like The BuzzBurger are listed on the left side, while a bunch of sandwiches fill the right. Beverages and a couple of desserts are on the back. I settle on a chicken Dijon sandwich and a diet soda.

I drop my menu onto the table. Chris has obviously decided what he wants, because he's already put his menu down. I'm not even sure he looked at it. He's been here before and probably knows what he likes.

A tall waiter with short black hair threads his way over to our table. He's wearing a loose light blue button shirt with the sleeves rolled up and black pants.

"Have you two decided what you want?" he asks, bending at the waist so he can hear our replies over the din.

I order my chicken sandwich and soda, and Chris orders a cheeseburger and a soda. We decide to split an order of fries. The waiter scribbles it down on a small pad.

"Shouldn't be too long," he says before spinning away and heading toward the kitchen.

"So," I say to Chris. "You were saying you were going to do what up on stage?"

He laughs. "Nice try. But I'm pretty sure I wasn't saying any such thing."

I feign a pout. "Oh, my bad. I thought you were."

"What's the matter? Don't you like surprises?"

"Sure I do. But only when I know what they are."

Chris laughs again. "I'm pretty sure that's not a

surprise, then."

"Oh." I smile sweetly. "I guess I don't like sur-prises, then." Cautious girls usually don't. I change the subject. "So, how many times have you been here for this open mic thing?"

"Just a couple of times near the end of last semester," he says. "This is the first time this year. And before you ask, no, I didn't sing, or tell jokes, or recite poetry."

So much for changing the subject. I decide I may as well go with the flow.

"Pole dance?" I ask.

"Ha, ha! You wish." He puts an exaggerated thinking expression on his face. "You know, maybe that's not such a bad idea," he says. "No one's done that yet."

I'm spared from having to come up with some smart retort by the arrival of our food.

"You two need anything else?" our waiter asks after putting our food, drinks and a bottle of ketchup on the table.

Chris looks at me, and I shake my head. "We're good," he says.

He picks up the ketchup and mimes pouring some onto the fries, which are the thick, plump kind I like, looking for my approval. I nod my head yes, so he shakes a couple of big blobs of ketchup onto the fries and then some more onto his burger.

I spear a fry with my fork and take a bite. It's warm and crispy, with just the right amount of salt. Very good, really. Chris picks up his burger in both hands and takes a big bite, his blue eyes smiling at me over the top of the burger. I smile back and bite into my sandwich. It's also very tasty. The Dijon sauce is just right and the chicken is nice and tender.

We don't talk too much while we're eating, which is fine with me. I hate having to worry about whether I've got food stuck in my teeth when I'm talking and eating at the same time.

"Did milady enjoy her dinner?" Chris asks when I finally shove my plate to the side.

"Immensely," I reply, making a show of delicately dabbing my lips with the paper napkin. "The cuisine was superb, the atmosphere enchanting, the service exceptional. I can't wait for the entertainment."

Our waiter comes over and grabs our plates. Did I mention he's pretty cute? Not that I noticed, of course.

Chris scoots his chair around the table so that he's next to me, facing the stage. Our timing is perfect, because some guy in the same blue shirt, black pants outfit as our waiter has just stepped up onto the stage and grabbed the microphone. He taps the mic with his fingers and then waits for the crowd to quiet.

"Welcome, everyone, to open mic night at The Joint," he says. Some whoops and whistles erupt from the crowd. "We're going to start with our traditional opening act," he continues when the whoops subside. "Give it up for one of your favorites, Tony Phillips!"

The whoops and whistles are louder this time and are joined by lots of applause. This guy must have a lot of fans here tonight, or maybe it's just a boisterous crowd ready to let loose and have some fun. The cheers continue as a chunky, dark-haired guy steps up onto the stage. He's carrying his own guitar, a much newer and nicer one than the instrument leaning against the wall. As he slips the strap over his head, the lights gleam off the shiny wooden face of his guitar. Then the overhead lights dim and he begins to play. I recognize the opening chords of Toby Keith's "I Love This Bar" immediately.

His voice is deep and masculine. "We got winners, we got losers, pot smokers and boozers. We got freshman, we got juniors, and we've got *lots* of slacker seniors."

He's changed the words to fit the college scene and the crowd is loving it. When he gets to the chorus—"I love The Joint"—the place erupts. The noise doesn't die down completely all the way through the song, and when he belts out his final "I love The Joint," the place explodes into thunderous applause. Chris is right. This *is* fun!

The MC jumps back onstage and grabs the microphone. "Tony Phillips, folks!" he says as the applause finally fades. "Thanks for getting us started, Tony. And as always, The Joint appreciates the plug."

Phillips waves to the crowd and steps down off the stage. He takes a seat at a table right in front with three other people seated at it.

"Our next performer is another regular here at The Joint," the MC continues. "You know him and you love him. Let's hear it for the always popular Stefan Handlemenn!"

More cheers break out as a slender blond guy wearing a black leather bomber jacket and a military cap steps up on stage. Some of the kids are shouting something that sounds like "ga...ga" over and over.

The guy takes a moment to set up a music player on a small table, fiddles with the controls briefly, and then stands with his back to the crowd. A driving electronic dance beat begins to blast from the player. The rhythm is familiar, but I can't place it. Handlemenn bends forward and does something with his cap, then spins around. The crowd erupts. Under the cap, he's now wearing a platinum colored, page-boy style wig.

He launches into a surprisingly good impression of Lady Gaga's "Paparazzi." The audience loves it, joining in with a rambunctious "papa-paparazzi" whenever he reaches the chorus. By the time he finishes, a bunch of people are on their feet, dancing. Have I mentioned how much fun this is?

The MC gets back on stage. "Thank you, Lady Gaga…uh, I mean Stefan. Wasn't that something, folks?" The crowd roars once again. "Now, who's brave enough to follow that performance?"

Chris looks at me and fakes like he's going to stand up, then sits back down and grins.

"No way would I go on after that," he says.

I'm still not sure whether he's serious about performing, or just having fun with me. I think I'd prefer he just stay seated here with me.

The next couple of people to step up onstage are a mixed bag. Two women sing—they're ok, but not great, and a guy tells some jokes. One or two of the jokes are pretty funny, but most are pretty lame. The crowd laughs and groans and applauds appropriately.

Then the guy in the wild plaid sports jacket takes the stage. His appearance is met with a few groans—I don't know if it's for his outfit or because they've seen him before. He pulls the microphone from the stand and walks to the very front of the stage.

"Is everyone having a good time tonight?" he asks. There's not much of a response, but he pushes on. "Did you hear about the guy on the track team who won a gold medal? He was so proud he had it bronzed." He waits for a reaction, but except for a few groans, the audience is silent. He seems to like the groans. I guess any reaction is better than no reaction.

"I had a date with a very hot blonde the other night," he says. "I don't want to say she wasn't smart, but later on, when things were getting hot and heavy, I blew in her ear. She said 'thanks for the refill.'"

The groans take a little longer to sound this time, as people try to figure out the joke. But when they come, they're even louder. A couple of kids laugh, though, and the guy smiles proudly. He stays onstage another couple of minutes, telling more jokes about students and about blondes, but the airhead one was the high point of his act. He receives a smattering of polite applause when he steps down from the stage. I'm not sure if he's lucky or not that people can't drink in here.

Before the MC even reaches the microphone, Chris is on his feet.

"Now that's an act I can definitely follow," he says. "Wish me luck."

Uh, oh. He's really going to do it. My mouth says "good luck," but my brain is saying "oh, no."

## CHAPTER 15

I feel myself slinking down into my chair as I watch Chris weave his way between the tables to the stage. *Relax, girl*, I tell myself—no one except the kids sitting right by us knows which table he came from. Besides, Chris is a smart guy. He wouldn't do this if there was any chance he might bomb—would he?

I force myself to sit up straighter. I wonder what's he's going to do? Not tell jokes, I hope. He's pretty funny sometimes, but this crowd seems much more into music than comedy. He's right about one thing, though—he's picked the perfect act to follow.

To my surprise, Chris doesn't get up onto the stage. Instead, he takes a seat at the piano. I definitely did not see that coming!

I have to admit, he looks pretty cute sitting there at the piano with that fedora on his head. It doesn't hurt that his sneakers are out of sight under the piano, either, at least from everywhere but the very front tables. I'm worried this is not a piano music kind of crowd, though. It could be worse, I guess. He could be playing the flute or the violin.

The MC looks over at him. "Well, it looks like our

next performer is ready," he says. "What's your name?"

"Chris."

"Okay, Chris. Do you need the mic?"

Chris shakes his head no. So now I know he's not going to sing. Or tell jokes. He's just going to play. I wonder what kind of music he plays?

The MC sticks the microphone back into the stand. "All right," he says. "Let's see what Chris has in store for us." He steps down from the stage.

Chris cracks his knuckles in front of his chest as the MC disappears into the crowd. He nods his head a couple of times—establishing a beat in his mind, I guess—and begins to play.

He starts slowly, barely touching the keys. The tune is somber, and hauntingly familiar. The low hum of conversation in the room begins to quiet, as people strain to hear the music. I don't think most of them know whether they like it or not yet. Chris begins to play louder, more forcefully, and I finally recognize the song. It's "Hurt"—the Trent Reznor version more so than the Johnny Cash. I can hear the lyrics in my head now. The music grows more powerful, and the room grows quieter. His playing isn't perfect, but it's pretty darn good. Maybe one day he and I will play a duet together—in private, of course. Never, ever in a place like this. My grandmother always tells me to never say never, but in this case....

Suddenly, the melody changes. Chris's fingers are pounding the keyboard now and his head is bobbing up and down. Without missing a beat, he's shifted from "Hurt" to "Whole Lot of Shakin'" by Jerry Lee Lewis. Talk about a leap. When his fingers slide across the keys in a loud glissando, the crowd roars.

"Go get 'em, Jerry Lee," someone yells. "Yee-haw!"

Chris bangs the keys for another few moments, then lifts his right foot from beneath the piano and begins bouncing his heel on the keyboard, playing the high notes with his foot. Along with most of the rest of the crowd, I laugh and I cheer. Now I know why he wore those crazy sneakers.

Finally, he finishes with a flourish, sliding his fingers along the entire length of the keyboard three times in row. The crowd cheers and whistles. He stands up and bows to the audience with a quick nod of his head, then begins to thread his way back through the tables, back toward me. He's grinning, but there's a touch of boyish shyness in his grin. It's the first sign of shyness I've ever seen in him. I kind of like it.

I'm still clapping softly when he sits down next to me. I can't believe I was worried he might bomb, and that I'd have to share in his embarrassment.

"Not bad," I say. "Not bad at all."

"Twelve years of lessons," he explains. "Mostly church music, show tunes and classical stuff, but when I learned my assignments well, I was allowed to have some fun."

"Well, you sure looked like you were having fun tonight, especially when you did that thing with your foot."

He grins. "Too much?" he asks.

I shake my head. "Definitely not. Just right for this place. They loved you."

"I told you, it's all in who you follow."

"Yeah, but being good helps, too," I say.

"So you really thought I was okay?" he asks.

I think it's cute that he still wants reassurance, even after the audience's reaction.

"Better than okay," I say. "Way better."

He wipes his brow with a napkin. "I was a little worried. I haven't played in a while."

"How come?"

He shrugs. "No piano. This is the only place I know that has one, except for the music department, and no way am I going to play there in front of all those genius types."

Those "genius types" may have done a shade better on "Hurt," perhaps, but no way would they have topped his Jerry Lee.

"So is this why you brought me here?" I ask. "So you could show off for me?"

He laughs. "We're here because I knew we'd have fun. Showing off was a bonus."

"Well, I'm duly impressed."

We listen to a bunch more acts. Some are pretty good, but only one gets a reaction anywhere near like the one Chris got, a teeny little girl with a big voice who did a great cover of Taylor Swift's "Back to December." She definitely had me believing she had treated some guy really crappy and now was very sorry. I wonder if guys ever feel that sorry about treating a girl badly. Probably not.

Around ten o'clock, we decide we've had enough. It's cooled down a few degrees outside, but the night air is still very pleasant. I slip my arms around Chris's arm as we stroll away from The Joint. The noise from inside fades as we get farther away.

"That was really fun," I say. "Thank you."

"My pleasure," he says.

"You realize, don't you, that anytime we go back there now, they're going to want you to play."

A surprised expression crosses his face and he stops walking. "Oh, I don't know about that."

"I do. I'm going to have to share you with all of them from now on." I smile. "I just hope you don't have a weakness for groupies."

He purses his lips like he's deep in thought, and then takes the fedora off his head and grins.

"I know," he says. "I won't wear this next time. Nobody will recognize me without it, and we won't have to worry about any groupies."

I laugh. "You're probably right." I nudge his foot with mine. "Especially if you don't wear these sneakers, either."

"Okay, got it. Next time, no hat, and lose the sneakers." He puts the fedora on my head and looks at me appraisingly.

I do a quick spin for him. "How do I look?" I ask, batting my eyelashes flirtatiously.

He puts his hands on my shoulders. "Really cute," he says, his voice serious now. "Like always."

His eyes are fixed on mine. My cheeks grow warm. Has the temperature of the night just gone up? I think I want to move my eyes away from his, but I must be wrong, because they stay glued there.

Uh, oh. His face is moving closer to mine.

Have I mentioned that we haven't really kissed yet?

A few light kisses on my cheek and a couple of goodnight pecks on the lips. That's been it. But I'm pretty sure that's about to change.

Am I ready for this? Truthfully, I don't know. In some ways, I am sooo ready. More than ready. But in other ways, I'm nowhere near ready. Cautious girl versus growing up college girl, I guess. I haven't kissed a boy for real since Brian, almost four years ago. My heart is pounding, threatening to burst out of my chest. Is it longing? Or fear? I'm pretty sure it's some of both. And if I'm going to do this, do I want to do it here, out on the street, where people can see? At least I won't have to worry about it going any further than a kiss out here. That's something, right?

I wonder what my face looks like right now. Like a deer in the headlights, probably. Surely Chris can see that, can't he? Then why is his face still getting closer?

I'm amazed at how many thoughts can race through my head in the time it's taking his lips to move toward mine. Is he moving in slow motion? Or has time just somehow slowed down?

But slow motion or not, it's about to happen, unless I do something to stop it. I know—I'll close my eyes. That'll stop it for sure, won't it?

But it doesn't stop it. I feel the warm taste of his breath on my lips an instant before his lips meet mine. They linger there, lightly, like a feather. A soft, moist, warm feather. A sweet, delicious feather. If I'm going to stop this, I need to stop it right now. But why on earth would I ever want to stop this? It's heaven.

Slowly, almost imperceptively, the pressure of his

mouth on mine increases. Words cannot describe the feeling. It's almost as if our lips are falling together, merging somehow, until I don't know where my lips end and his lips start. Time has not only slowed, I think it's stopped. And what a wonderful place for it to stop!

My heart is racing. His kiss is flawless, fearless. I feel his lips begin to open, pulling mine open with them. His tongue presses lightly against mine, and a current like a jolt of electricity shoots through me, all the way down to my toes. An odd thought pops into my head. I can feel my toes, but I can't feel the ground beneath them. Somehow, I'm floating, weightless. How is that possible? *Stop thinking, girl. Turn off your brain and just enjoy!*

His arms wrap more tightly around me, pulling me into him. His tongue begins to move. Slowly. Deliciously. With no conscious thought, my tongue follows his lead, pressing against his. Our tongues begin to dance, slowly at first, probing, tasting, testing, and then faster as our heat builds. I feel his hands move into my hair, holding my head. Somehow, despite his grip, my head is spinning. It's just another of the many impossibilities I'm sensing right now.

How long it all lasts, I have no idea. Days? No, of course not. That's ridiculous. But hours at least, right? Finally he pulls his mouth away. I wait a moment before I open my eyes, afraid that might break the spell. When I do open them, Chris' face is just a few inches from mine. He's smiling and his eyes are looking deep into mine. His hands are linked loosely behind my neck.

My heart is still racing. I try to come up with something clever to say. Or something romantic. But all that comes out is a soft "wow." *Oh, that's real good*, I tell myself. *Very creative.*

"Yeah," he says. "Wow."

I'm glad to see his brain isn't working any better than mine.

We stand like that—my arms around his waist, his hands behind my neck—for several more moments. We must look like a statue in a park—young lovers lost in each other. All we need are a couple of pigeons to complete the scene. I wonder if other girls feel like this when they get kissed, if they lose themselves so completely, so totally? Or is it something most of them get over in high school, but I never had the chance to get used to? I love the feeling—I hope I never get used to it. But it scares the hell out of me, too.

Finally, some guy across the street yells "Get a room!" His buddies laugh, like he's the first guy to ever come up with that one.

*Bite your tongue*, I want to scream as I drop my arms from around Chris's back. Getting a room is exactly what I don't want to do. At least, the part of me that thinks doesn't want to. A few of my other parts might argue.

Chris leaves his arms on my shoulders for another moment before pulling them away, plucking the fedora from my head as he does so.

Maybe it was the hat that cast that magic spell over me, like the hat that brought Frosty to life. That must be it.

"Let's walk," Chris says.

I take his hand. "Yeah, let's."

We stroll down the sidewalk. I notice we're not heading toward my dorm.

## CHAPTER 16

"You know," Chris says as we walk along the street, "I still owe you that tour of the Ritz."

My heart rate spikes and my grip on his hand tightens for a moment. Chris stops and looks at me. The hand squeeze was a definite giveaway. I don't think he expected so strong a reaction to his simple comment. But that's how I am. Always reading into things. This time, though, I'm pretty sure I'm reading them right.

How do I get myself out of this? And do I even want to get out of it?

I'm sure Chris has a pretty good idea about what's stressing me right now.

"What's the matter, Heather?" he asks. "Don't you trust me?"

Yep, he knows.

"No, it's not that," I say. "I do trust you." I give his hand a more gentle squeeze and smile. "At least, as much as I trust any of you horny college guys."

He laughs. "You know us guys too well."

"I'm just not ready for anything more yet," I explain. "Physically, I mean. And I'm not sure I trust myself to stop when I should. Can you understand?"

"Yeah, I can. I guess."

"I'm sorry to be acting like this," I say. "This is all so new to me."

"Really?" He looks genuinely surprised. "I'd have thought a girl as cute as you would have had lots of boyfriends."

"No," I say. "Not even close. Too careful, I guess."

"Why so careful? A bad experience?"

*Why so careful?* That's a question I'd need hours to answer.

"Not really," I say. I think of Gaby. "Not personally, anyhow. It has more to do with my mom and dad, I think. But I don't want to talk about them now. You'll understand when you meet them. If you're lucky enough to get that far, that is," I add with a grin.

He laughs. "That's not usually what guys mean when we say 'get lucky.' But don't worry, I'm cool with taking things slow—for a little while, at least."

"Thank you." I give him a quick kiss on the lips. "But I want to do more of that," I say. "Lots more." I can't believe I just said that. What happened to cautious girl?

He grins. "Maybe we need to find a chaperone, to make sure we behave ourselves."

I laugh. "I think Marissa would volunteer, for sure!"

"Let's head back to your place. If Marissa's there, she can watch us. If not, we'll make out in the hallway, where we can't get into any trouble."

I'm not sure if he's kidding or not. Or if I want him to be kidding. But we have to head somewhere, whether we're going to do more kissing or not.

"It's such a beautiful night," I say. "Can we take the long way back?"

"Sure. How about we go by the Student Center? That's definitely the long way home. There might even be something going on there."

"Perfect," I say.

We walk slowly, in no hurry, just enjoying the beautiful night and each other. Sometimes we hold hands, sometimes we let go when one of us reacts to a funny comment or needs to gesture to make a point. It's all so easy, and so natural. No stress involved. Not at all like that other stuff. Maybe that's why things were so easy with Justin—because we were just great friends. None of this sex stuff to worry about. I wanted to be more than friends with Justin, but I never got there. And I definitely want more with Chris. Luckily, it seems he does, too. Now if I can just get my head on straight.

Lots of other kids are walking around campus, some in pairs, some in larger groups. A few of the groups are loud and obnoxious, too much to drink at a party somewhere probably, but most of the kids are doing just what Chris and I are doing—walking and talking and having fun.

There's nothing special going on at the Student Center, but there's still plenty of students inside, grabbing a late snack or just hanging around with their friends. In front of the entrance, a bunch of kids are puffing on cigarettes, getting their nicotine fix before going back inside. Chris and I swerve onto the grass to avoid the cloud of smoke hovering over them.

"You ready to head home?" Chris asks. "We can cut

across the Green."

"Sure," I say.

The Green is a grass plaza bigger than a football field near the center of campus. We're at one end, in front of the Student Center. The other end is dominated by the library, a huge, cathedral-like stone edifice that's one of the oldest buildings on campus. Like the Student Center, the library is open twenty-four hours a day. A wide cement walkway connects the two. Two more sidewalks crisscross the plaza from corner to corner. The three walkways meet in the center, at a huge circular concrete fountain. A jet of water in the middle of the fountain spews ten feet into the air.

The Green is lit by a ring of lights fashioned to look like old-time gaslights, as well as a row of the same lights along each of the walkways, but the central area is still not as bright as the areas closer to the buildings. The grass triangles between the sidewalks are dimmer still.

Chris and I head down the central sidewalk toward the fountain. With each step, the noise from the Student Union fades and the night becomes a little darker, providing a sense of peaceful privacy. When we reach the fountain, the sound of the splashing water drowns out any remaining noise.

I'm about to ask Chris to stop here so we can watch the fountain for a few minutes, but before I can say anything, he puts his hands on my cheeks and kisses me. There's no time to get nervous or for questions to race through my brain. I simply dissolve into the kiss.

It's just as sensational as the first one. Maybe even better, since there was no worrying preceding it. There's nothing but the feel of his lips, the taste of his breath, and the urgent probing of his tongue. I surrender to the delicious feelings. Once again, time loses its meaning, and I know this sounds lame, but I think I see fireworks.

"Sorry," Chris says when he finally pulls his lips from mine. "I couldn't wait."

*Sorry?! Are you kidding me?* I want to tell him there's no reason to be sorry, no reason at all, but I'm still trying to catch my breath and engage my brain. I need to say something, or he's liable to think I'm mad at him.

"Umm, that's okay," I finally manage to say. *Oh, Heather, you silver-tongued devil, you.*

"I figured we couldn't get into any trouble out here," he says.

As if to emphasize the point, three girls walk past us on their way from the library to the Student Center. They barely give us a glance as they pass, but their presence gives my brain a chance to begin working again.

"It's not your fault I'm irresistible," I say, smiling. I bend to the fountain and splash a handful of water up at his face. "Maybe this will cool you off, though."

He tries to duck, but he's not quick enough. The water splashes against his cheek and drips slowly from his chin.

"And maybe this will cool *you* off, hot stuff," he says as he scoops me into his arms and threatens to toss me into the fountain.

"Nooo!" I scream, laughing. "Please don't! Pretty please!"

Oh, no, he's lifting me higher! He's not really going to throw me in, is he? He wouldn't!

He puts one foot up on the edge of the fountain and

balances my butt on his thigh. He's much stronger than he looks, cradling me in his arms with little effort. Before I can react, he's kissing me again. Oh, god, here come those fireworks again.

"We can still go back to my place," Chris says somewhat breathlessly when he finally pulls his mouth away from mine.

We're sitting on the cement rim of the fountain now. We've been kissing for awhile, and standing had become increasingly difficult, at least for me.

His simple declaration sets off a firefight in my brain. Part of me screams "yes!" while the careful part of me digs in with a firm "no way." Of course, Chris hears none of this, though maybe he can glimpse some of the internal struggle on my face. As the sensation of his lips against mine slowly fades, caution and common sense gain the upper hand, as they always do.

"Do you really think I'm any more ready now than I was a little while ago?" I ask, keeping my voice soft so he doesn't think I'm upset. "Because of a few more kisses?"

"No, not really," he says. He takes my hand in his and grins. "But I am."

I smile and shake my head. What am I going to do with him?

"Why am I not surprised by that?" I say.

"Sorry," he says. His grin is wider now. "I can't help it. I'm a guy."

"Well, Mister Guy, you're just going to have to learn to control yourself. Think you can do that?"

He grins again. "Do I have a choice?"

"Nope."

"Well, I guess that's settled, then," he says.

*Settled?* I wish the argument inside my head could be settled so easily. But at least Chris is being a gentleman about this. I just hope patience is one of his virtues, too, because I don't think I'm going to be ready for anything more anytime soon, despite the feelings swirling inside me. I wonder how long he'll be willing to wait? I wish I knew more about guys.

I think I need to have a long talk with Marissa.

## CHAPTER 17

**M**arissa is already in bed when Chris and I get back to my room. It's not quite midnight, so I guess it was an early Friday night for her. In a way, this is good. Chris and I share one more wonderful kiss outside my door, then we say goodnight. I don't have to worry about having him come in and being alone together in my room, and I also don't have to worry about what he might say to Marissa about having her watch us kiss. The boy can be such a wise guy sometimes.

I creep into the room as quietly as I can, after easing the door shut behind me. There's enough light filtering in through the windows and from the power indicators on all our electronic devices for me to see my way without turning on a light. I'm only halfway across the room when Marissa speaks.

"You can turn on the light," she says, her voice clear and alert. "I'm not asleep. I just got into bed five minutes ago."

I flick on my desk lamp, which still leaves her half of the room in dimness. I guess she really isn't all that sleepy, because she's already pushed her blanket down and swung her legs over the side of the bed.

"So, how was your date?" she asks.

"Really fun," I say. "I had a great time."

I sit down on my bed and tell her all about open mic night, finishing with Chris' wild piano playing.

"Jerry Lee Lewis, huh?" Marissa says. "That must have been something. I bet the place went wild when he started playing with his foot."

"They did. They loved it."

"So, did you two do anything else? Or was open mic night it?"

I smile at her. "Well, there might have been some making out involved afterward," I say.

Marissa leaps across the room and bounces onto the bed beside me. "All right! Let's hear it."

"I'm so glad you said that," I say. "Because I really need to talk to you about it."

"Uh, oh," Marissa says warily, sensing she might be getting into more than she bargained for. "I just wanted some good girl talk—you know, gossipy stuff. But that's not quite what you've got in mind, is it?"

"No," I say. "I really need some advice. I'm pretty clueless about this stuff."

Marissa grins. "Okay, I'll make you deal. Give me some juicy details first, and then we'll do the advice thing."

"I guess that's fair," I say. "But the details aren't all that juicy."

"Maybe not if they were coming from *me*," Marissa says, her grin growing wider. "But coming from my shy, innocent little roomie, they'll be plenty good."

I take a moment to decide where to start. I guess there's no place like the beginning.

"The first kiss was on the sidewalk, just outside The Joint," I say.

"The *first* kiss!" Marissa repeats. "That means there was more than one, then. I knew this was going to be good."

I tell Marissa about that first kiss, trying not to sound too sappy about it, but still getting across the idea of how amazing it felt. I leave out my lame "wow" comment when it ended. I finish by telling her how we just stood there afterwards, his arms draped over my shoulders, until some guy shouted the "get a room" thing. And how I panicked at the idea of that. And how it got even worse when he suggested we could go back to his room.

"I'm guessing that's what you want some advice about, huh?" Marissa asks.

"Yeah, kinda."

"Let's hear about those other kisses, before we come back to this. Okay?"

I tell her about the surprise kiss by the fountain, and how I splashed him, and how he picked me up and threatened to throw me into the water, but instead ended up kissing me again.

"If my math is correct, that's three major make-outs," Marissa says, grinning. "My little girl is growing up so fast!"

I feel myself blushing. I'm not sure if it's from the three make-out thing, or the teasing about how clueless and innocent I am. Probably both.

"After the third kiss, he mentioned going back to his

place again," I say. "That's when we had a little talk about how I'm nowhere near ready for that."

"Good girl," Marissa says. "Communication is totally important. At least that's what the grownups are always saying. What did he say to that?"

"He said he understood. But I think he was a little disappointed."

"Of course he was disappointed," Marissa says. "He's a guy. He's supposed to be disappointed. It's genetic."

"He said *he* was ready," I add.

"Whoa! Stop the presses!" Marissa is laughing now. "A guy who's ready for some nookie…who'd a thought it?"

I try not to laugh, but can't help myself. It is pretty funny, I guess. Especially from Marissa's point of view, I'm sure. And every other human being with an emotional age higher than twelve.

"I'm sorry," Marissa says when she stops laughing. "I know you're being serious. So what part of all this is bothering you so much? Did Chris try to push you into it?"

"No, not at all. He was a perfect gentleman. He even suggested we get a chaperone to watch us kiss, so we wouldn't get into any trouble?"

"A make-out chaperone? Now that *is* funny."

"I said I thought you'd volunteer for the job," I say.

"Totally!" Marissa says. "I'll make sure he keeps his hands where I can see 'em."

Now we're both laughing again.

"Chris sounds like he's cool with the way things are right now," Marissa says. "So, what's the problem?"

"He is cool with it," I say. "But I'm worried about

how long he'll stay that way. What if I'm not ready for anything more for a long time? How long will he wait?"

"If he really likes you, he'll wait as long as you need him to," Marissa says.

"I hope so," I say. "Because I really like him."

"Don't do anything until you're sure you're ready. One thing I know for certain—you can never go backwards. So make sure it's what *you* want to do."

I shake my head in resignation. "I'm so stupid about this stuff. Thanks for listening."

"Hey, no problem. And don't forget, until you're ready, I'm happy to chaperone."

## CHAPTER 18

Late Wednesday afternoon, Marissa, Katie, Beth and I are waiting in front of the dorm for my dad to pick us up and take us home for dinner. Mom and dad have been complaining I don't come home enough—duh, don't they know there's a reason for that?

I have mixed feelings about bringing my friends to my house. There's safety in numbers, sure, but do I really want to expose them to my parents? Mom and dad usually behave at least a little better with company around, but there are no guarantees. It will be a chance to show them I've made some good friends, and that's one of the reasons I spend most weekends on campus.

I've warned my friends my parents can be difficult, but they say it's no big deal—parents are supposed to be difficult. Marissa said it's part of their job description. Maybe so, but they don't know my mom and dad. But the girls don't really care—they're just looking forward to some home cooking. And my mom is a very good cook, I've got to give her that.

Oh, well. *Que sera, sera.* We'll see how it goes.

It's a bit cool this afternoon, so I'm wearing my gray

Old Navy zippered sweatshirt and jeans. Marissa has toned down her attire a bit for the occasion—"I don't want your mom and dad thinking I'm a bad influence," she'd joked. She's got on a pink hoodie with black and white checks running diagonally down one sleeve, hip-hugger jeans with no rips, and a pair of gray Nikes adorned with pink swooshes. Her "girly sneakers," she calls them. She's got four or five leather and bronze bracelets dangling from her right wrist to keep her from feeling "too plain." Katie's wearing a fuzzy, oversized powder blue sweater that hangs below her butt cheeks like a short dress, with tight black leggings and gray Ugg boots, while Beth looks preppie in a black argyle sweater with gray and white diamonds in vertical columns down the front, dark gray pants and black flats. She must really be trying to impress my mom and dad, because this is definitely not her usual look.

Dad pulls to the curb at precisely five o'clock, as promised. One thing I've got give the guy, he's punctual as all get out. He leaves the engine running as he climbs out of the Explorer and crosses around the front to give me a big hug. I hug him back, then pull free and introduce my friends.

"Nice to meet you all," he says. "Heather's told us all about you."

"Not *all* about us, I hope," Marissa jokes.

"Don't worry," I say, grinning. "Only the good stuff."

"Well, let's get going," dad says. "Heather's mom is eager to meet you all, too."

Led Zeppelin is singing about some lady who is sure all that glitters is gold as I climb into the front seat. The girls slide into the back, with Stacie getting stuck in the middle. My dad loves old rock music, so I've heard his songs forever, but I wonder if my friends even know who Led Zeppelin is.

The car smells deliciously of fresh-baked apple pie. Dad has obviously stopped at the bakery on the way here.

"Yum!" Beth says, breathing deep of the cinnamon-laced aroma. "Maybe we should have dessert first."

"You know what they say in the bakery business," dad says. "Life is short—eat dessert first. I'm not sure my wife would approve, though. She's making pizza."

"Double yum," says Beth.

Traffic isn't too bad, and we're home in less than twenty-five minutes. I lead my friends into the house while dad gets the pie out of the back. As soon as I step through the doorway, Sam is all over me, his tail wagging furiously. I drop to one knee and give him his favorite greeting—a vigorous chest rub. Once he's calmed down a bit, I introduce him to the girls. Marissa and Katie fawn over him, but Beth keeps her distance. I guess in addition to not doing woods, she doesn't do animals, either. Sam doesn't care. He's getting enough attention from Marissa and Katie to put him in dog heaven.

Finally, they straighten up, and I introduce them to my mom, who pulls off her spattered blue and white checked apron and hugs each of them.

"It's so nice to meet all of you," she says. "I hope we'll see you often."

"If that pie and pizza taste as good as they smell, Beth may never leave," Marissa jokes.

"You girls can take whatever's left back with you," mom says, laughing. "I hope the rest of you like pizza. It's obvious Beth does."

"Are you kidding?" Katie says. "What college kid doesn't?"

"My mom makes really good pizza," I say.

"Go ahead and sit," mom says, refastening her apron. "Dinner'll be ready in a couple minutes."

Marissa and I sit on one side of the table, Beth and Katie on the other. Mom has gone all out setting the table. She's put out an embroidered ivory tablecloth usually reserved for holidays, and is using her good sand-colored dinnerware and fancy silverware—for pizza, yet. Maybe she's hoping it will make dad realize this is a special occasion and help him be on his best behavior. There's a crystal goblet at each setting, and two tall red candles flicker in brass candlesticks a third of the way from each end. Sam isn't allowed near the table while people are eating, so he retreats to his favorite spot in front of the fireplace. After depositing the pie in the kitchen, dad joins us and sits at the head of the table.

A moment later, mom emerges from the kitchen with a big wooden salad bowl. She's gone all out with the salad, too. I can see tomatoes, green and red peppers, mushrooms, radishes and cucumbers all spread on a bed of Romaine lettuce.

Mom sets the salad down in the center of the table. "I don't know if you girls like salad," mom says, "but I'm sure your mothers will be happy I offered."

She disappears back into the kitchen, returning a moment later with three flasks of homemade dressing. "Balsamic, Italian and Ranch," she says, placing the bottles on the table. "Help yourselves."

Beth takes enough salad to be polite and passes the bowl Katie, who puts a healthy pile onto her plate. Marissa takes about the same amount as Beth and gives the bowl to me. I love salad, so I fill my plate.

"Pizza's on," mom says, carrying a rectangular wooden cutting board covered with a steaming pizza into the dining room. The aroma of spicy tomato sauce and pepperoni is much stronger now. "I hope you all like pepperoni, it's Heather's favorite. There's a mushroom pizza in the kitchen, if you prefer."

"Pepperoni is great," Beth says.

Mom sets set the pizza down next to the salad. "Diet cola okay for everyone? I have bottled water if you prefer."

We all opt for soda. Mom brings four cans from the kitchen, and we fill our goblets. Dad pours red wine for him and mom.

"To new friends," he toasts, lifting his glass.

We all clink glasses and then get down to the business of eating.

"Mmmmm, this is really good," Marissa says after her first bite.

"It's awesome," Beth adds. "Totally awesome."

"You should see what they try to pass off as pizza at the dorm," Katie says. "It's nothing like this, that's for sure."

Mom beams under the praise.

Conversation is pretty sparse as we concentrate on the pizza, which is just fine with me. Even dad has been unusually quiet. And with him, quiet is a very good thing. The first pizza disappears pretty quickly, so mom brings in the second.

"She may not be much to look at, but she sure can cook," dad says jokingly.

I feel myself stiffen. This is how it always starts. I see a fleeting look of pain cross my mom's face. She's actually pretty cute—for a mom, anyhow—with shoulder length strawberry blond hair that's a lot straighter than mine and a really nice smile.

"I guess you do like my cooking," mom retorts, "since there's twice as much of you now as there was when we got married."

Here we go. Dad's not anywhere near fat, but he does carry an extra ten pounds or so. In twenty years of marriage, my parents have learned exactly what buttons to push to achieve maximum effect.

Marissa seems to sense where this is heading, because she jumps in and quickly changes the subject. I wonder if her parents are anything like mine.

"Did Heather tell you she has a boyfriend," she says.

I'm grateful for the interruption, but I really wish she'd picked another subject—any other subject. I can feel myself blushing, and I'm tempted to kick her under the table. But she's managed to derail the impending train wreck between my parents, so I give her leg a break.

"No, she didn't," mom says. She looks at me and smiles. "Tell us about him, Heather. What's he like?"

"It's no big deal," I say, trying hard to downplay the whole thing. "I've only seen him a couple of times."

"He's a sophomore," Marissa says.

"And he's really cute, too," Beth adds.

"Then what's he doing with Heather?" dad asks,

grinning.

Oh Dad, you're just *so* funny. No wonder you've raised such a self-confident daughter. But I'm determined not to lash back. That's the mistake my mom always makes, striking back. At least I've learned *something* from all their bickering and fighting.

"How did you meet him," mom asks, ignoring my dad's comment about me. I wish she was as good at ignoring him when it's about her.

"Marissa shoved me into him," I say.

"Not quite into him, but close," Marissa says, grinning. "I could tell she wanted to talk to him. She just needed a little push. Tell them the rest of the story, Heather. It's pretty funny."

So I tell them about the red, blue, green, black thing, and how he came back at me with a string of colors of his own. They both laugh.

"That *is* pretty funny," mom says. "I bet your were so embarrassed when those colors came out of your mouth."

"Totally," I say. "I was looking around for a hole to climb into. And it gets worse. I told him Marissa pushed me, but when I turned around to point her out, she was gone. I was afraid he was going to think I was a crazy woman."

Marissa is grinning big time now. "I'm always glad to be of service in the course of true love," she says.

"Well, I'm glad it's working out so far," mom says. She looks at me. "It's been awhile since you've had a boyfriend, hasn't it?"

*Awhile?* Earth to mom. How about four years, Mom? I'd say that qualifies as awhile. And please don't ask *why* it's been so long. You wouldn't like the answer.

"All this talk about romance is making me hungry again," Katie says. "That pie's calling my name, I think."

I smile at her. She's doing her best to rescue me, I know. I'm so glad I warned them what my parents can be like. They're all doing a really good job handling the situation and protecting me. Good friends are definitely a good thing. A very good thing.

"Dessert's a great idea," dad says. "I'll get the pie."

The rest of the evening passes about the same way. There are a couple of close calls, but no major explosions. Now my parents know I've got some great friends—and even a boyfriend, thanks to Marissa—and my friends got a small taste of what my mom and dad are like. All in all, I'd call that a very successful evening.

Since it's a school night, we're able to leave early without seeming anxious to get out of here. What parent could argue against their kid wanting to get back for some studying? And did I mention how delicious the pie was?

# CHAPTER 19

College is not all fun and games, and dates and kisses, I am reminded quite clearly when midterms week arrives. I've been studying like mad all week, sleeping little and playing even less. I'm pretty sure I did well on my first three tests, but algebra tomorrow is going to be the toughest by far. My head is filled with equations and theorems. Luckily, Professor Simpson doesn't believe in exams—instead, we have to write a paper on one of the vampire books we've read so far. It's not due until the end of next week, so no pressure there. So after my algebra midterm, the crunch will be over—until finals, anyway. Ugh!

At least I'm not the only one feeling stressed. Girls have been wandering the halls like zombies, wearing no makeup, their eyes bloodshot, vacant looks blanking their tired faces. Yellow light leaks under doors and soft music filters through the walls at all hours of the night as many kids pull all-nighters. I've been up until the early hours twice already this week and will be putting in an even later night tonight. It's nearly one o'clock, and I'm still at my desk, pouring over my algebra workbooks. Lots more to go, too.

Even Marissa has been kind of subdued this week, joking more than once she wished she'd bought stock in Red Bull. Caffeine and herbs can do only so much, though, and she's showing the effects of the late hours. She's lying on her stomach on her bed right now, studying for her history midterm. Three empty cans of Red Bull on the floor by the side of her bed show how long she's been there.

I had my first Red Bull ever at the beginning of the week, and I'm now downing a couple of cans a night. I'm pretty sure some of the other girls in the dorm are using something stronger than energy drinks and coffee, but Red Bull is more than enough for me.

On top of everything else, I've only seen Chris once this week. He's as busy studying as I am, but we text each other every night, so that's something, at least.

The numbers on the pages are beginning to blur. I rub my eyes, but it doesn't help. I think it's time for a short break. I stand up and am immediately reminded how long I've been hunched over my desk—my spine creaks and protests like I'm eighty frigging years old. I force my shoulders back, trying to stretch the muscles in my upper back, and then slowly roll my neck in small circles. I decide to get out of the room for a bit.

"Taking a break?" Marissa asks, looking up from her book.

"Yeah. My eyes are getting blurry and my back's killing me," I say. "I'm going to take a walk around the dorm."

Marissa shuts her book and gingerly swings her legs

over the side of her bed. She's moving like I was when I first stood up.

"I know the feeling," I say sympathetically as Marissa stands up and stretches her arms over her head.

"A walk sounds like a great idea," she says. "Want some company?"

"You bet. Let's go."

"This sure ain't like high school, huh?" Marissa says as we head out the door.

I shake my head. "Not even close."

"I never stayed up past midnight in high school—not studying, anyhow," Marissa says, grinning.

"And I never drank Red Bull until this week," I say. "I guess college is all about new experiences."

"Yeah, but I'm liking some of those experiences better than others." Marissa stifles a yawn. "Just one more day, and this particular experience will be over." Her face brightens. "Then we have the big Halloween party next weekend. That'll be fun."

"I hope so."

"Miss Enthusiasm strikes again," Marissa teases.

It's pretty quiet in the hallway. Everyone's door is closed, and the only music playing is soft and muted—studying music. Most of the doorways glow with a telltale yellow strip at the bottom that says, "Yep, we're still up studying." There's no light showing under Katie and Beth's door, though.

"Katie's sleeping, lucky girl," Marissa tells me. "She's some kind of braniac. Beth says she never studies past midnight. Gets all A's and B's, too."

"And here we are, prowling the hallways at one

139

o'clock, with more studying still to go," I say, sighing. "I'd love to be in bed right now. Where's Beth? Don't tell me she's sleeping, too."

"Nah, she's pulling an all-nighter at the library. She says if she stays here, it's too easy to get distracted or to go to bed."

"Distracted like walking the halls?" I say, laughing.

Marissa grins. "This is a break, not a distraction. There's a difference."

"Okay. Let's walk down to the third floor, then the second. We can see if any of our dorm mates are freaking out. Then it's back to the grind."


I close my Blue Book and take what feels like my first real breath in almost two hours. I still have five minutes left for the exam, but I am done—sooo done. I think I did pretty well, though. At least a B—definitely good enough for algebra. All my studying paid off, thank god. I'm glad I got up early, too, because one of the problems on the test was something I studied this morning. Now I just want to go home, maybe take a nap.

I walk my booklet up to the front and drop it on top of the few others already there. A couple of math geeks have been finished for a while, but most of the kids are still frantically scribbling in their booklets as the final minutes tick away. The professor, a preppy blond guy in his late thirties, nods and gives me a small smile—my reward, I guess, for finishing early. I smile back sweetly before turning and heading for the door. It never hurts to do a little flirting with the teacher!

The bright sunny day grows brighter still when I see

Chris smiling up at me from the bottom of the steps. He's wearing jeans and a black waffle knit T-shirt with a small "No Fear" logo above his heart. Maybe if I got a shirt like that I'd have less fear in *my* heart. I should be so lucky.

Seeing Chris here is a total surprise, and a nice one. My fatigue seems to melt away as I hurry down the stairs.

He gives me a quick peck on the lips. "Hi, gorgeous," he says. "I see you survived the math monster. How'd you do?"

"I done good," I say. "The monster's gone, at least for now. Let's hope it stays that way for awhile."

"How about I take you to lunch?" he asks. "As a reward for making it through midterms."

"Great. I'm starving. I didn't have time for breakfast."

"Anywhere special you want to go?"

"Let's just go over to the Student Center. It's the nearest place with food." I smile. "Not great food, I grant you, but definitely edible."

"Sounds good to me. Let's go."

He takes my hand and we head around the corner toward the Student Center, which is only a block away.

The dining hall inside the Student Center is cavernous, furnished with plain, utilitarian plastic chairs and square wooden tables that can be pushed together to accommodate groups of any size. The rear wall is almost all glass and looks out onto the Green. I find myself smiling as I remember our wonderful night out there by the fountain. The cafeteria-style food service section is to our right. It's dominated by a long glass-covered counter stocked with sandwiches, salads, vegetables and side dishes. Behind the counter at the far end, a giant grill sizzles with hot dogs and hamburgers.

We cross to the food line. Ever the gentleman, Chris grabs two red plastic trays and hands one to me. He does the same with silverware and napkins. The line is short and moves quickly, with most of the kids skipping past the salads and veggies and heading straight for the sandwiches, fries and burgers. The smell of grilled beef and fries beckons me, even here at the far end of the counter.

I'm way too hungry for a salad today, and I don't want to waste time picking out salad fixings anyway. A burger and fries will do just fine, thank you. More than fine.

There's no wait at the grill, because this time of day the cook just keeps slapping burgers onto the sizzling grill, knowing how fast they'll disappear. Less than five minutes after we entered the building, Chris and I have gotten our food, grabbed two sodas, and found a table by the huge rear window. The din from dozens of animated conversations fills the place, but it's not too bad. I squirt some ketchup onto my fries and burger, and then offer the bottle to Chris.

I know it would probably be polite to wait until he's done getting his food ready before I start eating, but I'm too hungry. I grab my burger and take a big bite. As usual, the meat is cooked a bit too much, but as hungry as I am, it tastes great. Ditto with the fries—they're underdone and a little soggy, but that doesn't stop me from enjoying them.

A few bites of burger and a couple of fries take the edge of my hunger, and I slow down a bit. Chris is holding his burger in two hands in front of his mouth, watching me. It looks like he's only taken one bite so far, so he must not be nearly as hungry as I was. He seems to be looking at me a little bit funny, and I wonder if I have ketchup on my face or something.

I put my burger down and wipe my face with my napkin. Nope, no ketchup. It must be something else. Maybe the way I was wolfing down my food. Note to self: eat more lady-like.

"Is something wrong?" I ask.

He looks startled, like he didn't realize he was staring at me. "Umm…no. Why?"

"You were looking at me kind of strange," I say.

He takes a drink from his soda before replying. "Strange? What do you mean?"

"I'm not sure if I can describe it. It just felt like you were looking at me a little hard, maybe. I thought I'd smeared ketchup on my face or something."

"Sorry," he says. "I didn't mean to make you uncomfortable." He grins. "I just like looking at you. You're pretty cute."

I smile back. I'm finally getting used to him saying stuff like that, and even better, I'm starting to believe he means it.

"Thanks," I say. "You're not so bad yourself."

We both go back to our food. The rest of lunch goes just fine, but I can't rid of the feeling that something is wrong. It's nothing I can put my finger on, just a feeling that won't go away. Maybe I'm just tired from so much studying. I hope so. God knows I could use some sleep.

## CHAPTER 20

Friday morning I sleep in. It's been a long, tough week of studying and test taking, and I need the sleep. I deserve it, too. Just like I deserve the dinner Chris is taking me out for tonight.

It's after ten o'clock when I finally throw back the covers and swing my feet over the side of my bed. My eyes feel like someone rubbed sand in them and my mouth tastes like I've been chewing on a dirty sock. I think I have a Red Bull hangover.

"Welcome to the land of the living," Marissa says.

She's lying on her bed, dressed in black sweat pants and a gray T-shirt, reading a book. Her hair is damp. When she sits up, I see the front of the shirt is covered with a bright green design that looks like someone threw fluorescent paint at her.

"Ugggh," I say, rubbing my eyes. "I'm not sure I qualify as alive just yet. How long you been up?"

"Not long. Maybe forty-five minutes. When I woke up, I felt like you look right now." She lifts an empty can of Red Bull from the bed. "One of these plus a shower did wonders. Want me to get you one?"

"No. Thanks. I'm going to stay away from that stuff for awhile. I don't think I do caffeine very well. What are you reading?"

She holds up my copy of *Breathless*. "This thing is pretty good. I hope you don't mind me borrowing it, but I wanted something quiet to do while you were sleeping. And I didn't want to go *near* any of my textbooks."

"No problem," I say.

I haven't read *Breathless* yet, but I'm glad to hear it's good.

"I think maybe I'll sign up for that vampire class next semester," Marissa says, "even though there's hardly any guys in it."

I laugh. "You'll love it," I tell her. "Professor Simpson is pretty cool."

I force myself to my feet and grab a bottle of water from our mini-refrigerator. I take a mouthful and swish it around inside my mouth. The cold water feels awesome—I can almost feel the parched lining of my mouth soaking it up. Finally, I spit it out into the sink and take a big swallow. I'm starting to feel human. I'm also kind of hungry. I turn around and find Marissa watching me.

"Have you eaten anything yet?" I ask.

"Just an orange," she says, nodding toward the small basket of fruit atop the mini-fridge.

"I'm going to take a quick shower, then how about we go down and get some breakfast?"

"Sounds good," Marissa says.

Now that I'm starting to wake up, I'm beginning to pick up a strange vibe from Marissa. It feels like she's looking at me a little strangely. I wonder if I'm imagining

145

it. What the heck is going on with me? First Chris, and now Marissa. I really am becoming paranoid. Maybe I really do need to stay away from Red Bull.

I definitely need that shower, that much I know. I put on my terrycloth robe, grab a towel, and head down the hallway.

When I get back from the shower, Katie is sitting on Marissa's desk chair. Like Marissa, she's dressed for hanging around the dorm comfortably—dark blue leggings and light blue T-shirt. A column of dark blue diamonds runs down the right side of the shirt.

Marissa is sitting in her favorite spot, on the bed with her back propped on a pillow against the wall. She's still wearing her sweatpants and T-shirt. I know her well enough to know she's not going down to breakfast dressed like that. At eight in the morning if she's in a rush, maybe, but not at eleven.

Katie looks up at me as I enter. She's got a very uncomfortable look on her face. I *know* I'm not imagining that. What the heck is going on? Katie turns her face away from me and exchanges a glance with Marissa.

"What's going on, guys?" I ask.

"We need to talk to you, Heather," Marissa says. "Why don't you get dressed, then we'll talk."

I clutch my robe tighter around me. "You guys are creeping me out," I say. "What is it?"

"Get dressed," Marissa says softly. "Just throw something on. Anything."

I'm starting to get really anxious. I have no idea what's happening. Cautious girl does not like to feel in the dark like this. In fact, she hates it. For a moment, I think maybe I should go back into the shower and try this all over again. Or maybe go home and *really* start all over again.

I slip into the most comfortable things I own—a pair of dark gray sweats and a baggy black and white striped T-shirt. My wet hair begins to soak into my shirt, so I wrap it into a tight bun behind my head. It's going to look like crap when I let it down, but I'm beginning to think that's going be the least of my worries.

Neither Marissa nor Katie has said a single word while I dress. As soon as I get my hair up, I sit down on my bed. Without really thinking about it, I bring my legs up against me and wrap my arms around my shins protectively. I have a fleeting thought that maybe if I close my eyes, when I open them none of this will be happening. Maybe it's just a stress dream.

I should be so lucky.

"Well?" I ask. "What's going on?"

Katie looks at Marissa, who nods to her.

"I wasn't sure if I should tell you," Katie begins, "but Marissa said I had to. But not until midterms were over. We didn't want to mess up your tests."

*Not until midterms were over. Didn't want to mess up your tests.* Now I know this is going to be bad. But what the heck can it be? And do I really want to know? Didn't I read somewhere that "ignorance is bliss?" I'm all in favor of bliss right now. Lots and lots of bliss.

"Are you sure this is something I want to hear?" I ask, feeling like a condemned person praying for a stay of execution.

Marissa gets up and crosses the room. She sits beside me on my bed and puts her arm around my shoulders. Yep, this is going to be bad, all right.

"It's not something you'll want to hear," Marissa says gently, "but it's something you need to hear. Go ahead, Katie."

Katie looks like she'd rather be anywhere but here. God, do I know that feeling.

"It's about Chris," she says hesitantly.

*Chris!?* My mind starts racing. What about him? Is he alright? Has something happened to him? I just saw him yesterday, at lunch and at vampire class. He seemed fine. No, wait…I thought he was looking at me funny. Maybe I *wasn't* imagining it. Maybe he had something he wanted to tell me. Maybe he's sick. Oh god, don't tell me he's dying!

I try to rein in my thoughts before my imagination completely runs away from me. It can't be anything like that—why would Katie be the one telling me if it was? She barely knows Chris. No, it has to be something else. But what?

"I, uh, saw Chris Wednesday morning," Katie says. "Over at Clayton."

Clayton is a girls dormitory on the other side of campus. So what if she saw him there? Maybe he has a friend there, someone from one of his classes or something. Wednesday morning, no big deal. At least she didn't seem him there at midnight. But why is she telling me this if it's no big deal?

Somehow, I summon the courage to ask, "What was he doing?"

"He was, uh, leaving," Katie says. "I don't know if he saw me or not. Or if he knows I saw him."

*Leaving?* So what's the big deal? I was afraid she was going to tell me she saw him kissing someone, or holding someone's hand. There's got to me more to it. Uh, oh. What if…?

"Was he alone?" I ask, afraid to hear the answer.

"Yeah, he was alone."

I'm totally confused now. She saw him leaving a girls dorm, by himself. Why are she and Marissa making such an issue of this? It makes no sense.

"I don't get it," I say. "What's the big deal?"

"She saw him leaving at eight o'clock in the morning," Marissa says.

I look at Marissa for a moment, and then turn my eyes back to Katie.

"I was going over there to do some last minute studying with a friend from high school who's in my history class," Katie explains. "Chris was leaving one of the rooms. It was at the far end of the hall, and he turned the other way when he left. That's why I don't know if he saw me. But I think he might have."

I try to process all this, but my brain doesn't seem to want to work very well at the moment. Leaving a girl's room at eight in the morning—that doesn't sound good. No, not good at all. Was that why he was looking at me strangely yesterday? Was it guilt I saw on his face?

Katie is wringing her hands in her lap. She clearly doesn't want to go on, but she does.

"I asked my friend about the girl who lives there," she says. For a moment, she is silent, but I know there's more.

"She said the girl is the dorm slut," she says finally.

My heart drops as the picture completes itself. *Oh, Chris, how could you do this to me?* I feel Marissa's arm tighten around my shoulders.

"We wanted to make sure before we told you anything," Marissa says, "so Katie's friend talked to the girl who lives in the room next to the one Chris was leaving." She pauses for a moment. "She said she heard them doing it. She was sure of it."

The tears explode out of me. I can't breathe. I can't think. I twist around and bury my face against Marissa's shoulder, sobbing.

## CHAPTER 21

How long I cry I have no idea. It feels like hours. Time doesn't only stop for kisses, I guess. It stops for heartbreaks, too. Which really sucks.

Finally, I pull my face away from Marissa's shoulder and wipe my eyes with the back of my hand. I don't think there's a drop of water left inside me. I wonder if it's possible to cry every bit of moisture out of your body. Maybe that's why I feel so thirsty all of a sudden.

I've left a big wet spot on Marissa's shirt. I rub it gently with my fingers, as if I can somehow wipe it away.

"Sorry," I say.

Marissa keeps one arm around my shoulders and places her other hand gently on my forearm. "Don't worry about it," she says. "Are you okay?"

*No, I'm not okay* I want to scream. *Not anywhere near okay.*

"Not really," I say. "I feel...empty."

"Can I get you anything?" Katie asks.

She has a sad, guilty look on her face. I know she didn't want to tell me about this, but deep inside me I'm glad she did. Before I went and did something *really* not careful.

"Some water, maybe," I say.

The look on her face eases. I think she's glad to be able to do something to help. She gets a bottle of water from the mini-fridge and twists the cap off before handing it to me.

"Thanks," I mumble.

I take a small sip. It's hard to swallow, but I force myself to take one more sip before I hand the bottle back to Katie. She puts it down on my desk.

I have no idea what to do now. My brain doesn't seem capable of finishing a thought, and my body feels almost numb. I know something bad has happened, but it's almost as if it happened to someone else, someone separate from me. I've never felt so helpless, so detached. I don't want to move. I don't want to talk. I don't want to think. None of my fairy tales ever ended like this. I wouldn't let them.

Katie is standing in front of me, shifting her weight uncomfortably from one foot to the other, not sure what do to now. Welcome to the club.

But there's no reason for her to suffer, just because I am. Marissa, either.

"I think I want to be alone for awhile," I manage to say.

"Are you sure?" Marissa asks.

I nod my head. "Yeah. Please."

Marissa gives me a tight hug and then gets up from the bed. "We'll go hang out in Katie's room. If you need anything, just come get us. Or call, if you don't feel like leaving the room."

I nod again.

"I mean it," Marissa says. "We're here for you, Heather."

They head for the door, but Marissa stops by the fridge and grabs an apple from the basket.

"You said you were hungry."

She tosses the apple toward me. I manage to catch it, more in self-defense than out of any desire to eat.

"Try to eat something, if you can," Marissa says. "There's some cheese and yogurt in the fridge."

I paste a weak smile on my face, so they'll know it's okay to leave me alone. It's not much of a smile, but it's the best I can do. They look at me for a moment before leaving the room and closing the door softly behind them.

Now what? What do I do, now that I'm alone? Put on some music, maybe? Marissa turned her player off while I was in the shower. I guess she didn't want the wrong song to pop up while she and Katie were giving me the bad news. What would I want to hear? Certainly not one of my sappy love songs. That would be like twisting the knife in a wound. Maybe some my-heart-is-breaking song, like "Leave the Pieces" by the Wreckers, or something really tragic, like Pearl Jam's "Last Kiss." Or maybe one of the saddest songs ever written—"He Stopped Loving Her Today." They say misery loves company—but I'm not sure I want that kind of company.

I absently take a bite of the apple. I can tell it's moist and juicy, but I can't really taste it. I take another bite anyway, just to be doing something. If I had the energy, I'd get up and get some cheese to go with it, but that seems like too much effort for too little payoff. Now if there were some chocolate ice cream in the fridge, that might be a different story.

Finally, I decide to do what I always do when I need to escape. I get my guitar.

For a few minutes, I just sit on my bed with my guitar on my lap. The feel of its familiar weight on my legs is comforting—as comforting as anything can be now that my world has fallen apart. Eventually, I begin to strum the strings, tentatively, not playing anything, just making sounds. What song would I play, anyhow? Almost every song I know is a happy love song. I've no use for any of them now, no use at all. I wonder if I ever will again. I may have to learn a whole new set of songs. At least that will keep me busy.

The sounds rising from my guitar are not pleasant; how could they be, the way I'm feeling? For awhile, the chords are sad, plaintive, rising from a deeply wounded place inside me. Why did Chris have to go and break a perfectly good heart? I wish I knew how to write music—I bet I could write a killer broken heart song right now. Slowly, something changes, and the music begins to grow angry. My hand starts to move faster, almost attacking the strings with the pick.

I need to calm down. If I keep playing like this, I'll bust a string. But do I really care? What's a broken string compared to a broken heart? Broken stings can be replaced; I don't know about a broken heart.

But there's a part of me deep inside that loves this guitar and won't let me hurt it, no matter how bad I feel. Almost of its own volition, my hand begins to slow and the music grows softer. Before I realize it, I'm playing

"Teardrops on My Guitar." How fitting, I think, as a tear runs down my cheek and lands on the face of my guitar.

I play the song over and over, not singing—I couldn't even think of singing right now—just playing the sad music, until my fingers begin to grow cramped and sore and I can't play another note.

I put my guitar down beside me on the bed. Now what? I look around the room—it seems awfully small all of a sudden. I grab my partly eaten apple. The edges around where I've bitten have turned brown, but I take a bite anyway, just for something to do. It's just as juicy as it was before. And just as tasteless. I don't care. I eat the whole thing and then toss the core toward the wastebasket by my desk. It misses, but who cares? Not me. I leave it lying on the floor.

The room seems even smaller now, like the walls are slowly closing in on me. I need to get out of here, but where would I go? Marissa and Katie are down in Katie's room. I could join them there, but that doesn't seem any better. Worse in some ways, because they'd want me to talk, and I don't know if I want to talk right now. No, sitting around with them and not talking would feel even worse, I'm pretty sure.

But I need to do something. Maybe a walk will help. At least I'd be out of here, and I'd be moving. That's something. And something is better than nothing, right? I'll see if Marissa and Katie want to go. If we're walking, I won't have to talk if I don't feel like it.

I head down the hall. Katie's door is open, so I walk in.

They're sitting next to each other on Katie's bed,

looking at something on her laptop. Pink is singing. I recognize her voice, but I don't know the name of the song. They look up at my arrival, and Marissa jumps up off the bed and gives me a quick hug.

"How are you doing?" she asks.

I shrug. "I'm going to take a walk. You guys wanna come?"

"You bet," Marissa says. She looks at Katie.

"Yeah, I'll come," Katie says.

"Let's go then," I say.

Katie looks at me quizzically. "Like that?" she asks.

I follow her gaze down to my feet. I'm not wearing shoes or socks. I can't believe I hadn't even noticed.

"Oops," I say. "I guess I forgot something."

"Let's go back to our room," Marissa says. "Put on some walking stuff."

"I'll meet you there in a minute," Katie says. "I need to change, too."

Back in our room, I swap my sweatpants for a pair of black cotton sports shorts. It's a bit too cool out for just my T-shirt, so I put my lightest hoodie on over it, a tan one I can unzip if I get too warm.

I'm tying the laces on my Nikes when my phone buzzes. I reach for it automatically, but stop myself as soon as my hand closes around it. My heart starts beating faster. The odds are it's a text from Chris. I'm pretty sure I don't want to see it right now.

Marissa is watching me. I'm sure she's guessed it's from Chris, too.

"You gonna look?" she asks.

I take a deep breath. "I don't know. I don't want to." I

look down at the phone in my hand, then back to Marissa. "Do you think I should?"

"Aren't you two supposed to go out tonight?"

I feel my face tighten into a grimace. "Yeah, like that's gonna happen now."

"If he doesn't hear back from you, he's liable to just show up. Do you want that?"

Good question. My first thought is of course not, but then I think about having the chance to throw something at him and then slam the door in his face. There might be some mild satisfaction in that, but I think over all I'd rather never see his lying, cheating face again.

I flip open my cell. It's a text from Chris, all right, about our date tonight. My fingers type in a short message, and then I shut off the phone.

"That was quick," Marissa says. "What did you say?"

"Drop dead, asshole."

Marissa grins and embraces me. "Good girl," she says.

# CHAPTER 22

Marissa, Katie and I walk to the park. It's a beautiful day—sunny, temperature in the mid-fifties, barely a hint of a breeze. Puffy white clouds float lazily in a bright blue sky. Some of the leaves are beginning to turn, adding splashes of bright red and gold to the greenery. It's truly a magnificent vista.

But it's all lost on me. Any other day, I would have stopped for a few moments to drink in the beauty. But not today. Today I just want to keep moving. I have to keep moving.

We've been walking pretty fast. Neither Marissa nor Katie has said anything to me—they're waiting for me to speak first. I know when I'm ready to talk, they'll listen. Until then, they're leaving me alone. The silence is surely uncomfortable for them, but they don't seem to mind. I'm lucky to have such good friends.

We're halfway up the hill on the Lake Trail when I finally break my silence.

"Do you think it was my fault?" I ask softly.

Marissa stops. "What?" she asks.

"I said, do you think it's my fault?"

"Are you kidding?" Her voice is edged with anger. "No way was any of this your fault."

Deep in my heart, I know she's right, but I can't quite convince my brain of that. "Maybe if I hadn't needed to go so slowly…." I say.

I can see the fury building in Marissa's eyes. "What, you think if you'd put out a little bit, none of this would have happened?" she says. "You can't be serious."

"I know he wanted to do more," I say, not sure why I'm arguing the point, unless it's to punish myself a bit more. "Maybe if I wasn't so friggin' careful, he wouldn't have needed to, you know…."

"No, no, and no," Marissa says.

"It's not like it's been a year," Katie says, "but even that wouldn't be any excuse for what he did."

"I'm not saying I should have slept with him. But maybe we could have done more than kiss."

"For god's sake, Heather, it's only been a month." Marissa's voice is softer now. "If he can't wait any longer than that, he doesn't deserve you. He's a jerk, pure and simple. He cheated on you. Period. Don't you think for even a moment that any of this is your fault." She gives my forearm a firm squeeze. "If I hear anything more like that out of you, I'm gonna pound you. You got that?"

I can't help smiling. Amazingly, it feels good. "Yeah, I got it. Loud and clear."

We resume our walk. I still feel like crap, but at least a little less crappy than before.

By the time we get back to the dorm, I'm feeling mildly better. Not good by any means, not by a long shot. But a little better, and that's something.

Unfortunately, as soon as the elevator door slides open, all the good the hike did me is instantly undone.

Sitting on the floor next to my door is the last person I want to see. Chris. He's wearing that stupid fedora. He scrambles to his feet as soon as he sees us. Damn, he still looks cute. I hate myself for thinking that.

For a moment, nobody speaks.

"What are *you* doing here?" I say finally, putting as much venom into my voice as I can. "Didn't you get my text?"

He glances briefly at Katie. It's clear he knows she saw him and that she told me about it.

"Yeah, I got it." He takes his hat off and fumbles with it in front of his waist. As much as I can, I'm enjoying his discomfort. "I need to talk to you, Heather."

Marissa and Katie are watching me.

"What do you want us to do, Heather?" Marissa asks.

*What do I want you to do?* How about punching his lights out? Or cutting off his balls? Yeah, that might be a good start.

"Please, Heather," Chris says, "you have to listen to me."

No, I don't have to listen to him. What could he possibly say to make this right? But it's clear he isn't going to go away. I might as well get this over with.

I look to Marissa and Katie. "It's okay. I'll give him five minutes."

"We'll be right down the hall, watching," Marissa says. She fastens her eyes on Chris. "Don't even *think* of touching her."

Marissa and Katie move about halfway down the hallway and stop. Both of them stand there with their arms folded across their chests, watching us. If looks could kill, I wouldn't have to worry about dealing with Chris, for sure.

"I'm sorry, Heather," he says. "Really sorry."

My anger is becoming mixed with sadness. "How could you do that to me, Chris?"

"I'm so sorry." He shakes his head slowly. "It didn't mean anything, I promise. She doesn't mean anything. You're the one I love."

Tears are welling up in my eyes. I fight to keep them from flowing. "Maybe it didn't mean anything to you," I say, "but it means a helluva lot to me."

"She came on to me," he says lamely. "Big time. What was I supposed to do?"

*What were you supposed to do?* I can't believe he's asking me that. Guys really do live in a different universe.

"How about just saying 'No?'" I say, nearly shouting. "N - O. No."

Chris seems startled by my outburst. What was he expecting? That he would apologize and I'd melt and sweetly forgive him? As if!

"It didn't mean anything," he says again. "I swear."

The sad thing is, I believe him. But so what? That doesn't change anything. He can't take it back. Not ever. Some bells just can't be unrung.

"Did you think I wouldn't find out, Chris? Did you think that somehow I wouldn't mind? That I could overlook it?"

"I didn't...I mean, I wasn't…. Thinking, that is."

"Well, you should have thought. You should have thought real hard. And then you should have thought again… and again. That's what you should have done." I wipe my eyes with my hand. I've got my tears under control. "You just shouldn't have done it, Chris. That's all there is to it. You shouldn't have done it."

I can see tears filling the edges of his eyes. He looks like a little boy who just lost his dog. But tough luck—he dug this hole himself. I'm certainly not pulling him out. Not even a little.

"Go home, Chris. I never want to see you again."

I step past him and open my door. Without another word, I go inside and close the door behind me. I make sure to make plenty of noise putting the chain on the door, so he'll understand—it's over.

## CHAPTER 23

**I**'ve been in a funk all week. Breaking up is hard. Really hard. I wouldn't wish it on anybody. It just plain sucks.

I don't know if I was truly in love with Chris—I don't have nearly enough experience with that stuff to know. There's only so much you can learn from fairy tales and love songs. And this isn't a fairy tale, not by a long shot. And I'm surely not a princess.

But even if I wasn't in love with him, I definitely liked him an awful lot. And I miss him a lot, too. Marissa keeps pointing out—very gently, of course—that Chris and I were only together for a little over a month. God, if it feels like this after barely a month, how does anyone get through a breakup when they've been together way longer? I can't even imagine it.

Maybe I'm lucky I've only had two real boyfriends. And back with Brian, things just kind of dissolved, so there wasn't much pain involved for either of us. I guess being a cautious girl isn't so bad after all. In fact, maybe it's smart. Really smart. Why is everyone so eager to look for love, when it always seems to lead to heartbreak? Just ask Gaby. I guess there's a good reason there are so many broken heart songs.

Despite my grief, I dragged myself to all my classes, except for vampire lit. I'm not ready to run into Chris, so I skipped that one this week. I don't think missing it one time will affect my grade. I probably could have skipped all my classes, for all the good I got out of them. My concentration just isn't there. I try to listen, I really do, but my mind seems to have a mind of its own. Hey, that's pretty funny, right? My mind having a mind of its own? I wonder if that second mind also has a mind of its own. And maybe that third one does, too. This could go on forever, like when you look into a mirror with another mirror behind you.

See? This is why going to class has been such a waste. I can't concentrate on anything for more than a few minutes at a time, so most of what my professors say goes in one ear and out the other. My brain keeps taking off on these weird tangents. In my rare lucid moments, I recognize my brain is probably trying to protect me, taking me on these seemingly meaningless trips to keep me from going down more painful avenues. Marissa, Katie and Beth keep telling me it will get easier. They've all been through this. They promise me I'll get over him, that before long he'll just be another bad memory, just another picture to burn. I want to believe them. I really do. But right now it feels like I'll never get better.

I don't have any pictures of Chris to burn, but I've deleted every trace of his presence from my cell and from my computer. It hasn't really helped yet. I wish it were that easy to delete him from my heart.

\*    \*    \*

It's Friday afternoon. I'm sitting on my bed, my back pressed against the wall, trying to put a little space between me and Marissa, Katie and Beth. They're taking turns trying to talk me into going to tomorrow night's big Halloween bash. That I'm even considering going to what is billed as the biggest and wildest party of the year seems a big enough step for me, but apparently they're not going to let up until I say yes. They can be pretty relentless. Especially when they think it's in my best interest.

"C'mon, Heather," Marissa says. "It'll be fun, I promise. You've been moping around for a week now. You need to get out and have some fun."

Marissa has pulled her desk chair right up close to my bed—the better to pressure me—and Beth is hovering right behind her shoulder. At least Katie is nice enough to sit across the room instead of looming over me.

"Yeah," Beth says, "don't be such a wet blanket."

*Wet blanket?* Hey, I'll be a sopping wet blanket if I want to. Heck, I'll be a friggin' *drowned* blanket. But I don't think that's what my friends want to hear.

"Find me a party with no guys there, and I'll be happy to go," I say.

"Now what fun would that be?" Beth asks, grinning. "Halloween's the one night where even good little girls get to dress slutty. But what's the point if there's no guys around to see?"

*Dress slutty?* Is she kidding? Just thinking about going to the party is almost more than I can handle. No way am I wearing a costume that's going to make guys think I have even the remotest interest in anyone of their species.

"Is that supposed to make me *want* to go?" I ask. "Look guys, I'm not saying I'm going, but if I do, I am *not* wearing anything sexy or slutty. No way."

"But then what's the point?" Beth says. "I think…."

Marissa interrupts her. "Shush, Beth," she says, then turns back to me. "You don't have to wear anything sexy, Heather. Just dress up and have a good time with your friends."

"Yeah, Heather, c'mon," Katie says. "Marissa, Beth and me will wear the sexy stuff." She grins. "No guys will even notice you."

"Hey, that gives me a great idea," I say. "I'll go as the Invisible Woman. That way even you three won't notice I'm not there."

Marissa slaps me playfully on the shin. "C'mon, Heather, be serious. We want you to come. And don't worry about any guys. I promise at least one of us will stay with you every minute."

They're wearing me down, and I think they know it. Besides, I'm not really looking forward to sitting home alone in an empty dorm. But there's still one more problem. One very big problem.

"What if Chris shows up?" I say. "I don't think I could handle that."

"There's gonna be hundreds of kids there," Marissa says. "We might not run into him even if he is there. But if he tries to come near you, we'll keep him away, I promise."

"Yeah, we'll keep him away," Beth says. "Part of my costume is a whip. I'll use it on him if he gets too close."

I can't help smiling. He deserves a whipping, at the

least.

"A whip?" I say. "Who are you going as, Indiana Jones?"

"She's going as a dominatrix," Katie says. "You should see her outfit."

"Yeah," Marissa says. "Even I wouldn't be caught in that thing."

Beth grins. "I told you, Halloween's the one night we can wear anything we want. A girl's got to take advantage of it."

I've already seen Marissa's costume, and it's pretty slutty. She's going as a hooker. If she says she wouldn't wear what Beth is wearing, then it must really be something.

"What about you, Katie?" I ask. "What are you going as?"

"A nurse."

I'm surprised to hear that. "What's so sexy about a nurse?" I ask.

"You haven't seen her nurse's uniform," Beth says, grinning. "It's cut down to here and up to here." She uses her finger to indicate a spot just above her navel and another way up on her thigh.

I look at Katie, who shrugs and gives me a "what the heck" expression.

Okay, they're all going to look pretty sexy. So if I do decide to go, what can I wear to make sure I don't get any unwanted attention? No good ideas come to mind right away, but that's not a surprise, given the way my brain's been working—or rather, not working—lately.

"All right," I say. "I give up. You guys are impossible

to say no to. I'll go, but on one condition. We have to come up with a costume I'm comfortable with."

"Awesome!" Marissa says. Done pressuring me, she slides her chair back a foot or so from my bed.

"Maybe we can find you a nice gorilla suit or something," Beth says. "As tall as you are, everyone'll think you're a guy."

Marissa and Beth laugh. I don't really think we're going to find a gorilla suit, at least not one I can afford. But I like the way she's thinking, and I say so.

"A gorilla costume would probably be too hot to wear, even if we could find one," Marissa says. "The party's inside. You don't want to bake in your costume."

"How about a zombie?" Katie suggests. "We can make you as ugly and disgusting as you want."

*Ugly and disgusting?* I like the sound of that. Not only are zombies totally not sexy, but they're also really popular, so I bet there'll be lots of them at the party. I'll blend in with all the rest. Camouflage, safety in numbers, and all that. Maybe this party won't be so bad after all.

"Okay. I think I can probably handle being a zombie. Let's do it."

"Great!" Marissa says. "We'll go down to Goodwill to get some clothes we can shred, and then pick up some fake blood at the costume store. It'll be fun, Heather. You'll see."

I'm not really convinced it will be fun, but at least it shouldn't be too bad. And right now, not too bad is about all I really can ask for.

## CHAPTER 24

The night air is cool as we head to the party. A firm breeze out of the north chills our faces, and I wonder if there's a storm on the way for tomorrow. The forecast for tonight is dry, though, so we don't have to worry about raincoats or umbrellas, or worse, having the rain ruin our carefully applied Halloween makeup. It's only four or five blocks to the old facilities warehouse, so we're walking. We've all got hoodies over our costumes, but I'll bet Marissa and Beth are still chilly in their skimpy outfits. I'm plenty comfortable in mine, though—I just hope I continue feeling comfortable throughout the party. And I don't mean temperature wise, of course. I'm still not one hundred percent certain of my decision to go to this thing.

Halloween isn't for another couple days, but Saturday night is always a big party night, so there are a bunch of Halloween bashes on campus tonight. We pass lots of costumed students going in every direction. Some of the groups are pretty loud, so they must have started partying early. Most of the kids are heading in the same direction we are, because by far the biggest of the parties is the one we're going to. Three fraternities have joined together to host it, and word is they've been decorating the place for almost a week.

As we come around the corner, I see a long line of costumed students snaking from the front of the old building, but luckily, we don't have to wait in that line. A guy Marissa went to high school with gave her passes that allow us to skip the line and go in through a side door open only to fraternity members and their guests. Three guys man the door, one from each of the frats, probably. One is tall and muscular, and is proudly showing off his physique in a leopard skin loincloth. He doesn't appear to feeling the cold. His skin is very tan, so he's either been hitting the tanning booth or he did some kind of spray on tan—it's too dark out here to tell which. The other two guys are dressed as a pirate and a vampire. I bet there'll be even more vampires than zombies here tonight. The more zombies there are, the better for me, though.

The guys check our passes and stamp the back of our hands with a black skull and crossbones design without bothering to ask for any proof of age. You don't have to be twenty-one to get into the party, but you do have to be stamped to get any booze from the bar inside.

Too bad I don't drink, I think as I admire the stamp. But Marissa and Beth do, and they're both grinning happily as we step into a small meeting room reserved for guests with the special passes. There's no one else in the room right now, but the place is cluttered with coats and sweatshirts piled atop tables and hanging from metal hooks on the wall. In here, I can just barely hear the music from the band in the main room through the cement walls. We peel off our hoodies and hang them on top of one another on an empty hook in the corner.

"Look out, guys," Beth says. "The hotties have arrived."

Well, three hotties and one zombie, anyhow.

Beth's dominatrix outfit is totally over the top. The main piece is a tight black leather corset that shoves her boobs up almost to her chin. Katie said it took her ten minutes to lace Beth into the thing. I'm afraid to ask if Beth bought the corset for the occasion or if it's part of her regular wardrobe. Besides, I don't really want to know the answer to that one. Beneath the corset, dark red fishnet stockings extend into a pair of ankle-high black boots with four-inch stiletto heels. Her eyes are dark with gobs of purple shadow, and she's painted her lips with dark red lipstick to match her stockings. She's got a small whip attached her hip by a metal ring on her corset, and she's holding a leather riding crop in her right hand. She snaps the crop suggestively into her palm every few minutes, getting into the part.

Marissa makes an especially slutty hooker in a tight gold lamé top worn with black leather hot pants. Gold lace garters hold up black fishnets at mid thigh. Her black eye shadow—even thicker than Beth's—is flecked with gold sparkles, and her lips are painted a bright, garish red. She's added a blond streak down the left side of her hair to match her already blonde tips. A black spider web tattoo— henna, thank god, not real ink—covers the right side of her neck.

Compared to Marissa and Beth, Katie looks almost virginal. She's dressed entirely in white. She's unbuttoned the shirt of her nurse's uniform almost to her waist and her white shorts are hemmed so high they're barely wider than a belt. White tights cover her slender legs, and a pair of white sneakers and a small white cap pinned demurely atop her head complete the outfit. Somehow, she looks both proper and dirty at the same time.

My zombie costume couldn't be more different in tone from theirs. I'm wearing a ripped pair of jeans—not stylishly ripped, more like shredded—and a similarly decrepit black and white flannel shirt. I got the pants and the shirt from the Goodwill store for only a couple of bucks each, so we really went to town tearing them up. My hair's tucked up under a white bandana stained thoroughly with fake blood. We emptied the bottle of the stuff onto the shirt and the jeans, so I'm one bloody zombie. No reason to save the blood for another day.

I smeared my face with a layer of beige foundation so light in color it's almost white, and blackened a couple of teeth with stuff we got from the costume store. Marissa finished my look by painting two streaks of fake blood down from the corners of my mouth. There's nothing remotely sexy or provocative about my costume—except to another zombie, maybe. And that's exactly how I want it.

Marissa, Katie and Beth take advantage of the privacy of the room to do some last minute primping and to make sure their costumes cover—and don't cover—their bodies exactly the way they want. When they've all passed one another's inspections, we leave the room and cross the hallway into the party.

The frat guys have really gone all out decorating the cavernous old warehouse. Black and orange sheets cover most of the windows and the walls, and giant cobwebs festooned with skeletons, headless corpses and hairy black spiders dangle from the high ceiling. Huge painted orange pumpkins with scary faces glare at us from the black sheets; black pumpkins with equally frightening expressions adorn the orange ones. A five-man rock band in the front of the huge room was is pounding out Oingo Boingo's classic "Dead Man's Party," the first of several times they'll play the popular Halloween anthem tonight. A couple of hundred costumed students already fill the place, but there's room for many more. In front of the band, dozens of kids are dancing wildly to the raucous music. The back of the room, where four long tables serve as a bar, looks almost as crowded. The center is less packed, but there're still plenty of kids milling about, talking and laughing and checking each other out.

I'm amazed at the variety of costumes here tonight. Just from where I'm standing, I can see at least a half-dozen vampires and zombies, a couple of pirates, and assorted devils, hookers, black cats, French maids, princesses and serving wenches. One vampire, already surrounded by a cluster of fawning girls, looks amazingly like Robert Pattinson from the Twilight movies. I'm pretty sure he's one guy who won't be going home alone tonight.

As Beth predicted, the majority of girls' costumes flaunt their bodies in one way or another. The whole place oozes sexuality. *Carpe diem.* If you got it, flaunt it. I'm feeling better by the minute—there's more than enough exposed flesh to keep the guys occupied and away from me.

Before we're more than a dozen feet into the room, a

trio of guys cut us off. One's dressed as a vampire, complete with a black cape and plastic fangs. His face is even whiter than mine. The second is a bearded pirate wielding a plastic cutlass, and a third is a pretty cute guy wearing a horrible powder blue tuxedo that looks like something left over from a very bad wedding. I guess he knows he's cute enough to get away with a totally funky costume. The guys make no attempt to hide their appreciative stares. Thankfully, none are directed at me.

"Hello, gorgeous ladies," the vampire drawls through his fangs. "Anyone up for a bite?"

I barely stifle my groan. Anyone smart enough to get into State should be able to come up with a more original line than that.

"Only if *you're* up for a spanking," Beth counters, slapping her crop into her palm.

Tuxedo guy and the pirate laugh, while the vampire gives Beth a closer look. "That just might be fun," he says, his eyes lingering on her tight corset.

The pirate moves closer to Marissa. "I like the cut of your jib, wench," he says. "Methinks you and me might make a pretty good pair. What say you to a bit o' burning and pillaging together?"

Marissa looks at me and rolls her eyes. I know exactly what she's thinking—these guys are trying way too hard. I want to say that's what you girls get for dressing like that, but I hold my tongue.

"Sorry," Marissa says to the pirate as she circles her arm around mine. "As you can see, my zombie friend here's in pretty bad shape. I need to hang with her."

"What about you?" tuxedo guy asks Katie. "Do you

have to take care of her, too? Or can they spare you for a dance or two?"

Katie looks at me and I nod. As long as Marissa stays with me, I'll be fine.

"Sure," she says to tuxedo guy. "One dance." She grins. "Two if I like you."

"What about you?" the pirate asks Beth. "Wanna dance?"

"Sure, why not?" She slaps her crop emphatically into her palm. "But you'd better behave yourself."

The pirate laughs. "Or?" he asks teasingly.

"Or I might *not* spank you," Beth says without missing a beat. "Let's go." As she strides away toward the dance area, she puts an extra wiggle into her walk. The pirate hurries after her.

"Looks like you're odd man out," Marissa says to the vampire. "But don't worry. I'm sure there's a neck around here somewhere with your name on it." She turns to me. "I'm thirsty. Let's get a drink."

"Okay," I say. "Nice to meet you," I say to the vampire. "Good hunting."

We pick our way through the crowd toward the bar, and manage to make it almost all the way across the room before we're stopped again, this time by a guy in a colorful clown costume, complete with a frizzy red wig. He glides smoothly into our path and points at the blood streaks on my chin.

"Cut yourself shaving?" he asks. He squeezes the ball of an old-fashioned horn stuck in his belt and doubles over, guffawing in exaggerated clown laughter at his joke.

While he's bent over, we swerve around him and

continue toward the bar. The closer we get, the thicker the crowd becomes. We inch our way to the far right end, which is reserved for people with skull stamps, and has a line barely a third as long as the others. It turns out our stamps not only mark us as old enough to drink, but also as guests of one of the fraternities. The less fortunate kids have pumpkin stamps and have to wait in the longer lines.

"It's definitely not what you know, but who you know," Marissa says with a grin as we move to the shorter line and fall into place behind guy in a foam bodybuilder costume.

"Well, I'm sure glad I know you," I say. "The girl with connections."

In just a few moments, we reach the front of the line. All the bartenders are dressed as pirates. The one serving our line happens to be Frank, the guy who gave Marissa the passes. He's wearing a billowing white shirt, baggy black pants, and knee-high black leather boots. A black tri-cornered hat slants rakishly above his unshaven face, and he's got a stuffed green and yellow parrot perched on his shoulder. He grins and nods approvingly at Marissa's outfit.

"You look great," he says. "Very sexy."

"Hi, Frank," Marissa says. "This is my friend Heather."

"Nice to meet you, Heather," he says. "I like your costume, too. It's one of the better zombie getups I've seen so far tonight."

"Thanks for the passes, Frank," Marissa says, holding out her hand and displaying the skull and crossbones stamp. "They're awesome."

"No problem," Frank replies. "So, what can I get for you lovely lasses?"

I ask for a Diet cola and Marissa orders a rum and Coke, which Frank mixes quickly in a clear plastic cup.

"Arrrrrrrgh," he said in a pirate brogue as he drops a wedge of lime into the drink. "Yer a lass after me own heart, Marissa." He lifts the bottle of rum in front of his lips and starts singing in a gruff voice. "Fifteen men on the dead man's chest, yo ho ho and a bottle of rum."

"Don't quit your day job, Frank," Marissa advises him with a grin.

"No way," Frank says. "How would I afford your fee if I did?" He gives Marissa a big wink. "What's your hourly rate?"

Marissa grins. "You know what they say, Frank, if you have to ask, you can't afford it."

Frank grins back. "Oh, well. Can't blame a guy for trying."

I feel almost invisible standing there sipping my soda as Marissa and Frank banter back and forth. And I don't mind it at all. This zombie thing is working perfectly.

"Catch you later, Frank," Marissa says as we edge away from the bar to give the people behind us a chance to get a drink.

"You doing okay, Heather?" Marissa asks.

"Yeah, fine," I say. "This costume was a great idea. Nobody's paying any attention to me at all. Especially with you around, hot stuff."

Marissa smiles and thrusts out her chest. "Glad to be of help," she says.

We stand around for a couple of minutes, chatting and

checking out all the other costumes. Some of them are really pretty creative. One guy is dressed up as a bottle of wine, complete with a corkscrew sticking up straight up out of his head!

I spot Katie and Beth heading our way. Tuxedo guy and the pirate are nowhere in sight.

"Whatcha drinking?" Beth asks Marissa. Marissa hands her the cup and Beth takes a sip. "Mmmm, rum and Coke. I think I'll get me one of those."

We all get back in line, Beth and Katie to get a drink, me and Marissa to keep them company while they wait.

"Where are the guys?" Marissa asks. "You throw them back already?"

"Grant was pretty nice," Katie says. "And a good dancer, too. I gave him my number, but told him I had to get back to my friends."

"I threw mine back," Beth says. "I think he was a little too interested in having me spank him."

We all laugh.

The line moves pretty quickly, and before long Beth has her rum and cola and Katie is sipping from a cup of orange juice. Before we leave the line, Frank tops off Marissa's drink with a splash of rum and a bit more soda.

"No sense leaving the bar without a full glass," he says.

"That's what I call service," Marissa says with a grin as we move away from the bar. "Maybe I should dress like this more often."

"Do you really think that pirate guy was kinky?" I ask Beth.

"Yeah, I do. He kept staring at my crop and my

whip." She puts her hands under her half-exposed breasts and lifts them. "You'd think he want to stare at these," she says, "but no."

We all laugh again.

"Let's go dance," Katie says. "The four of us. The band's pretty good."

"Yeah, we don't need any guys to have fun tonight," Marissa says.

I realize they're all looking at me, hoping the "wet blanket" has dried out enough to have some fun. I shrug my shoulders and smile.

"Sounds good to me," I say. Before any of them can move, I'm heading for dance area. "Well, what are you guys waiting for," I call back over my shoulder. Wet blanket my butt!

We find some open space at the edge of the dance floor, just as the band starts playing "Monster Mash," by Boris somebody and the Cryptkickers, I think. I first heard this song when I was five or six years old and I've loved it ever since. The bouncy rhythm, offbeat lyrics and weird voice of the lead singer make it my favorite Halloween song.

The four of us start bouncing to the beat. I'm not doing any regular steps—I'm just letting my body move loosely to the music. Katie and Beth seem to be doing the same, but Marissa looks like she's actually following some routine.

"Try this," she tells us, almost yelling to be heard above the music. "My grandmother taught it to me when I was a kid. It's the official Monster Mash dance."

We stop and watch her for a few moments. The arm

movements are pretty easy—she's just kind of flailing them about—but the stuff she's doing with her feet is more complex. She's sort of pivoting on the ball of one foot, then raising the other, then reversing the move. It takes me a couple of tries to get it down, but before the song is halfway done, I've got it. I'm bouncing and pivoting and flailing like a mirror image of Marissa. Beth and Katie are doing the same on either side of me.

Before long, I notice a bunch of the kids around us are copying our moves. We've got a whole packet of Monster Mashers going now.

When the song ends, someone shouts, "Play it again!" More kids take up the chant, so the band obligingly plays an encore. We're now ringed by kids doing the Monster Mash.

We're all feeding off one another's energy, dancing wildly and singing the lyrics out loud. It feels really great to let loose like this.

Okay, I'm officially having a good time. Maybe there is life after Chris.

## CHAPTER 25

Yes, there is life after Chris. It's not as much fun—there are no head-spinning, heart pounding kissing moments— but it's a whole lot safer. And safer is just fine with this cautious girl. More than fine.

It helps to have really good girlfriends, which is something I didn't have in high school, at least after Gaby moved away. Marissa and I spend lots of time together, hanging out, hiking, going to the movies and such, and Beth is around a bunch, too. She often joins us for the indoor stuff. Katie has started dating Grant from the Halloween party, so she's not with us as much, but we still see her a lot, especially around the dorm. She says Grant's really fun and really nice. I hope so.

Beth got a Wii from her parents for her birthday last week, and we've all been having fun playing *Guitar Hero*, rocking out and pretending we're rock stars. I like being able to let loose and "play" guitar with other people around, even though the thing is just a plastic toy and doesn't even have strings. One night there were eight girls from the dorm taking turns at the game, three at a time.

I finally played my guitar again for Marissa the other

day, just a couple of songs. She said I was pretty good, and she felt very honored when I told her she's the only person I've ever played for. I still won't let her tell anyone else that I play though, not even Beth and Katie. If they knew, I'm sure they'd both want to hear me play, and I'm not ready for that.

I've been teaching myself some new songs. No broken heart songs—I don't need to make myself feel sad, thank you—and no love songs, either. I know too many of those already, and I'm not really in the mood for fairly tales. And it seems to me that's just what love is—a fairy tale. I don't think it truly exists in the real world, not that I've seen, anyhow. So I've been looking for fun songs. Alan Jackson's "It's Five O'clock Somewhere" is a good one, even though I don't drink. So is Jimmy Buffet's "Cheeseburger in Paradise." How can you not like a song with lyrics about lettuce and tomato, ketchup, and French fried potatoes? There's not a mention of romance or heartbreak anywhere in either of those songs. And cheeseburgers will never let you down, either.

My brain is working again, and I'm doing well in my classes, enjoying them all except for algebra, which is still a major pain. I've seen Chris twice, from a distance in vampire class. There's still some hurt when I see him, but it's getting a little better each time. I always make sure to sit between two people—girls, of course—so he has no chance to come sit by me even if he wanted to. I hustle out of class as soon as it's over, too. I'm taking no chances with any unwanted encounters. So far, he hasn't tried anything like ambushing me at the door, for which I'm thankful.

Tonight, I'm going to my first frat party, with Marissa. It's a "Thirsty Thursday" party she got invited to by a guy in her history class. I hesitated when she first brought it up, thinking why go to a party like that if I don't drink and I'm not interested in trying to meet a guy—and believe me, I'm not—but then I remembered how much fun I had at the Halloween party a couple of weeks ago. So I figure, why not? There'll be music, I can dance with Marissa, and it's only a few blocks away, so I can leave anytime I feel like it.

Now if I can just figure out what to wear. Marissa says I should wear my hunting outfit, but I told her I am most definitely not hunting, and I don't want to wear anything that will make the guys think otherwise. I almost wish I could dress up as a zombie again—that outfit kept the guys away just fine!

I put on a red and gray diamond-patterned skirt Marissa and I found at The Buff. It looks pretty cute, in a nice chaste kind of way, which is exactly what I want. The problem is, I have no idea what to pair it with.

"C'mon, party girl," Marissa says from across the room. "We don't have all night."

She's finished dressing already, and she looks hot. She's wearing the shirt with the diagonal rows of skulls and hearts and the frayed edge she bought that first time we went to The Buff. She's got it unbuttoned farther down than I would ever dare, and she's paired it with a short black skirt that sits low on her hips and red fishnets ripped in several places. Black platform shoes add almost four inches to her height. I'm not sure I could even stand in those shoes, much less walk in them. But she manages just fine. Practice makes perfect, I guess. A lower center of gravity probably helps, too.

"Help me out," I plead. "I don't know what to wear with this skirt."

Marissa crosses over to my closet. "Let's see what you've got," she says as she begins rummaging through the hanging clothes.

"I want to look nice, but *not* hot or sexy," I remind her. "I don't want to give any wrong signals."

"Don't worry, we'll save sexy for me," she says, grinning. "The plainer we make you, the hotter I'll look by comparison." She pulls out a gray tie-neck top with a scalloped bottom edge. "Try this."

I slip into the top and check myself out in the wall mirror. Perfect. Prim and modest looking, but stylishly so. Definitely not bait for any of those wild frat guys. I add a pair of plain black flats to complete my outfit.

"I think we're ready to rock," Marissa says.

I'm not sure how ready I am to rock, but maybe I can roll a little bit. We each grab a coat and head out the door.

It's pretty cool out, but we're not going far and the coats are more than enough. The moon is visible only as blurry glow behind a layer of gauzy clouds. Marissa's heavy shoes clomp loudly on the sidewalk—we definitely won't be sneaking up on anybody tonight.

I hear the festivities before we even turn the corner onto Fraternity Row. The thumping dance music seems almost to vibrate the sidewalk, and the tumult of voices and laughter is nearly as loud. Anyone heading for the party won't need directions to find it, that's for sure. The frat house is white with green trim, located near the center of a string of huge wooden houses that make up Fraternity Row. Three big green Greek letters—delta, psi and epsilon—are attached above the raised front entrance. Light is spilling from all but one of the dozen or so front windows. The one dark window on the third floor stands out like a missing tooth in a bright smile. I don't even want to think about what might be going in that unlit room.

Just in case someone can't tell where the party is, there's a bed sheet painted with giant green letters proclaiming "Thirsty Thursday" flapping in the breeze beneath one of the upper windows. Outside, a small crowd of kids is milling about on the front lawn and sidewalk, but the bulk of the noise is coming from inside the old house.

Marissa grabs my arm and heads toward the front steps. A short line of kids fills the stairs, waiting to show ID to receive the precious hand stamp marking them as old enough to drink. I bet once you're inside, it probably doesn't matter whether you're stamped or not. Not at a party like this one. Still, they're going through the formality, probably to keep Campus Security off their backs.

"Remember," Marissa says while we wait in line, "don't drink anything unless you pour it yourself, or if someone gives you an unopened can. Some of these frat boys will do anything to get you naked, including drugging your drink."

"Don't worry," I say. "It's diet soda or water for me."

"Unopened," Marissa repeats. "They can drug a can of soda as easy as a glass."

It's not like I don't know that, but I appreciate the way she's looking out for me.

The two guys flanking the doorway at the top of the stairs are definitely upperclassmen, cute in a preppie sort of way. They're confident in their manner and look to be enjoying their position of authority, especially since the line is almost all girls. Both guys are wearing casual tan sport coats open over black T-shirts. One guy's shirt has an old-fashioned white peace symbol on it; the other's says ORGASM DONOR in red block letters. I wonder if he bought the shirt because he thinks it funny, or because he thinks it will help him get some action. Neither choice is very flattering to him, but thinking it was funny would be the better of the two.

They give us practiced once-overs when we reach the top of the stairs. Orgasm guy flashes a wide grin.

"Good evening, ladies.," he says. "Welcome to Delta Psi Epsilon."

"Let me stamp your hand," peace symbol guy says, grabbing my wrist without even asking to see if ID.

I gently disengage my arm from his grip. "I don't drink," I say. I see a flicker of disappointment cross his face. This is one girl, at least, who will not be letting her guard down with booze.

"But I do," Marissa says, smiling and extending her hand flirtatiously.

The guy laughs and stamps the back of her hand. He holds his grip even after he's done, letting his eyes move up and down Marissa's body. I can tell she's enjoying the attention.

"I bet you do," he says, smiling. "Have a great time, girls."

We squeeze past the two guys and enter the house.

"This party's off to a great start," Marissa says, laughing and holding her arm out to admire the dark skull stamp on the back of her hand. "And look, the stamp matches my shirt."

Inside, the noise seems to have doubled. Pink's "So What" is blasting from unseen speakers, and loud chatter competes with the music. Frequent shrieks of laughter or shock—I can't really tell which—rise above the din. The room's filled with dancers gyrating wildly to the bouncy rhythm, and there seems to be at least four women for every guy. These frat guys definitely have a good thing going here. Little do they know, it's a good thing for me as well. The more girls there are, the less likely anyone will find the need to bother me.

Marissa and I pick our way through the crowd to the far side of the room, where the crush of people is less thick. Despite the open door and windows, the air is hot from so many bodies, so we find a couch to throw our coats onto. I look enviously at Marissa's mostly unbuttoned top and pull my own shirt away from my neck to let in a little air. At least my legs are bare.

A guy in what seems to be the standard Delta Psi uniform of sport coat and T-shirt moves confidently over to us. His T-shirt is dark brown and decorated with a grinning white Cheshire Cat face. He's cute in a not cute sort of way, with thick black hair and big brown eyes. His forehead glistens with sweat, and I wonder how warm the place will have to get before the frat guys' jackets come off. I bet they keep them on as long as they can stand, to let the girls know who they are.

"Can I get you girls a drink?" he asks.

"We'll get our own, thanks," Marissa replies. She smiles and puts her arm through his. "But you can take us to the bar, though."

The guy smiles back, then leads us into what seems to be a dining room near the rear of the house. Three frat brothers are busy mixing drinks behind a row of portable tables. A large plastic cooler contains cans of soda and bottles of water, while a second cooler holds cans of Red Bull and Monster. The booze is all behind the tables, out of reach. It's quieter back here, but not much, with a steady stream of kids coming and going from the makeshift bar. A bit of cool air filters in from an open doorway in the back of the room, but it's still plenty warm. I think cold water will be just the ticket right now, so I grab a bottle.

Marissa pulls a Red Bull from the cooler and hands it to our escort. "I'll have a Jagar Bomb," she says, smiling sweetly.

I have no idea what that is, but it definitely doesn't sound healthy.

The guy grins though, clearly pleased by her choice. "You got it."

"From a new bottle of Jagermeister, please," Marissa adds.

"Naturally," the guy says. "A girl can't be too careful nowadays."

I couldn't have said it better myself!

He grabs a plastic cup from a tall stack atop the table and reaches behind the bar for a dark green bottle of Jagermeister. He says something to one of his frat brothers behind the table, who hands him a shot glass. He pours a full shot of the dark brown liquor, and then fills the plastic cup a little more than half full with Red Bull. Holding the cup in his left hand and the shot in his right, he drops the shot glass directly into the Red Bull with a dramatic flourish and hands the cup to Marissa.

I grimace as she swallows the mixture in one long series of gulps. I'm definitely going to have to watch out for her tonight.

"Want another?" the guy asks as soon as she'd finished, his face a picture of friendly innocence.

"You wish," Marissa says, grinning. She holds out her hand. "I'm Marissa."

"Nice to meet you, Marissa," he says as he gallantly kisses the back of her hand. "I'm Andy."

"And this is Heather," Marissa says.

Andy kisses my hand as well, but I can see his eyes never leave Marissa.

He leads us away from the bar area back into a third room, still crowded, but less busy with people coming and going. What starts as a three-way conversation quickly morphs into an animated chat between Marissa and Andy, leaving me feeling a bit like a third wheel. But better no attention, than the wrong kind of attention. I'm happy to be ignored.

I spend a few minutes people watching. I'm surprised how many of the girls seem drunk already—it can't be any later than ten o'clock—and how many of them seem no older than me. I bet these guys are pouring really strong drinks. No wonder frat parties have the reputation they do. I'm glad Marissa said no to a second one of those bomb things.

I nudge her on the shoulder. "I'm hot," I say. "I'm going out back for some air."

"Want me to come with you?" she asks.

I shake my head. "No, stay here." I wink at her. "You look like you're having fun."

Marissa grins. "You sure?"

"Yeah, I'll be fine."

"Okay. Be careful, though." Marissa ruffles Andy's thick hair. "You gotta watch out for these frat boys."

I laugh and begin edging my way through the crowd toward the door.

The difference in temperature between inside and out is startling. At first, the cold is a welcome change, but before long I've got my arms wrapped across my chest trying to keep warm. I tough it out for another moment or two before giving up and heading back inside.

There's a Delta Psi guy leaning against the doorframe. I have a feeling he's been watching me. Why, I'm not sure, when there are so many hotter girls around. And drunk ones, too.

"Hi," he says as I walk by. "You having fun?"

I stop. I can't walk by without saying something. That would be rude. There's something familiar about him, but I can't place it. He's too old to be in any of my classes, a junior at least, I guess. But I don't know where else I could have seen him. He's kind of cute—not that I'm interested in that kind of thing, of course. Taller than me, with short, very blond hair and pretty green eyes. The dark blue T-shirt under his frat jacket is decorated with some kind of Asian symbol, written in gold.

"Not all that much," I say guardedly.

"Me neither," he says, then smiles. "I'm James. What do you say we not have fun together for minute or two?"

I laugh. He seems harmless enough, with no trace of the predatory air so many of his frat brothers give off. Besides, it'll give Marissa another couple of minutes alone with Andy. And James does have a really nice smile.

"Sure, why not?" I say. "I'm Heather." I hold out my hand. Thankfully, he shakes it briefly rather than kissing it. Score one point for him.

"So, Heather, what brings you to this not-so-fun party?" He glances back over his shoulder for a moment, nodding at the crowd inside. "You don't seem like most of the other girls here." He smiles again. "That's a compliment, by the way."

"Thanks," I say. "And yeah, I guess I am different from most of them. I don't drink, for one thing."

"I noticed," he says, looking down at my half full water bottle. "Good for you. I don't either."

I feign shock. "What? A frat boy who doesn't drink? Twitter alert! Newsflash!" I smile. "How'd you get accepted here if you don't drink?"

He laughs. "I lied. Told 'em I drink like a fish. They're all usually so drunk at these things they don't notice I'm not."

"So how come you don't? Drink, I mean."

He shrugs. "Gotta keep my grades up. I'm from a tiny little town you never heard of, and college is my ticket out of there. The only stoplight in town is a blinking one, and there's absolutely zero to do. Graduating is the only way to make sure I don't get stuck back there."

"I'm impressed," I tell him. "A guy who thinks about

more than how much fun can he have tonight."

"Don't be," he says. "If you ever saw my dad on one of his benders, you'd know how easy it is for me to not go down that road. He's another reason I want out of there for good."

I totally understand the wanting to get away from parents thing, though I don't want to be away from mine forever—just most of the time. But that's a more intimate conversation than I'm prepared to have. Apparently, it's not a topic he wants to get into either, because he steers the conversation back to very safe ground.

"How about you?" he asks. "You from around here?"

"Yeah," I say. "Right down the road. Less than ten miles from campus."

"Living at home, then?"

"No, I live on campus." I see no need to tell him which dorm.

He looks at me for a moment. I think he must suspect there's a reason I choose to live away from home even though it's so close, but he doesn't say anything about it.

"So, where's Jerry Lee tonight?" he asks.

*Huh? Jerry Lee?* What the heck's he talking about? He must have me confused with someone else. Maybe that's why he was watching me before. Yeah, that must be it. He thinks I'm someone else.

"Jerry Lee?" I ask.

"Yeah, the crazy piano player. The guy with the hat."

Oh…he's talking about Chris. He must have been in The Joint that night. I can see why he'd remember Chris— he put on quite the show—but why does he remember me? Maybe he saw us leaving together. Oh, god! I hope he didn't see us kissing outside!

"He's gone," I manage to say, trying to keep my tone flat and unconcerned. "History."

"Sorry to hear that," he says. He sounds really sincere. "You two looked good together."

"Well, not everything works out the way we want," I say.

"No, I guess not," he says. He has enough sense not to pursue the subject, for which I'm very grateful.

"I'd better get back to my friend," I say. "She's inside, chatting up one of your frat brothers."

"Oh? I hope she picked a good one. There's a few of them, but not very many."

I jump at the chance to learn something about the guy Marissa is clearly interested in.

"His name is Andy," I say. "Is he one of the okay ones?"

"Yeah, he's one of the good guys." James grins. "But don't tell him I said so."

I smile. "Your secret's safe with me. Nice meeting you, James."

"Same here, Heather."

And that's that. He lets me leave without trying to get me to stay, or even pestering me for my phone number. For a minute I think it's probably because he wasn't attracted to me at all, but he didn't have to say anything when I walked past, and he certainly didn't have to keep the conversation going. No, he seemed to like me, at least a little. I guess he could tell I'm kind of down on guys right now, so why waste his time. Still, I'm glad he let me go so easily. Not all guys would, I know, especially at a party like this.

I find Marissa and Andy right where I left them, chatting away. Marissa looks up at my arrival.

"Hey, Heather," she says. "You lasted longer out there in the cold than I expected."

"Not really," I say. "I got cold pretty quick. I was talking to some guy by the door for a few minutes. One of Andy's frat brothers."

"Uh, oh," Andy says. "Which one?"

"James."

"Oh, he's all right—for a guy who doesn't drink, that is. You don't have to worry about him."

I wasn't really worrying about him at all, but it's nice to know.

"Just a casual chat," I say. "Nothing more. I'm not in the market for a guy right now."

"That's cool," Andy says. He turns to Marissa. "What about you? You in the market?"

She wraps her hands around Andy's forearm and grins. "Oh, I'm *always* shopping," she says. "Are you for sale?"

"You bet," he says. "Or, you could just rent me if you want."

Marissa laughs. "Now that's a hard offer to pass up." She lets go of his arm and grabs mine. "I told Heather we'd do some dancing, though."

"That's okay," I say, not wanting to get in the way of what looks like a budding romance. "You don't have to."

"Yes I do," she says. "I want to make sure you have some fun tonight. I already gave Andy my number." She looks at him. "You'll call me, right."

"Definitely," he says. "Count on it."

"See?" she says to me. "We're all set. Let's go shake, rattle and roll."

So that's exactly what we do.

## CHAPTER 26

**I'**m lying on my bed on my stomach, reading that *Breathless* book for my vampire class. Taylor Swift's "Speak Now" CD is playing softly in the background. I love the sound of her voice, and I've finally reached the point where neither her sad songs nor her love songs hurt too much—as long as I don't play them too loudly or listen to the lyrics too closely, anyhow. Some of her lines are so poignant and still poke at me pretty good, like that kissing on the sidewalk thing in "Sparks Fly." That hits way too close to home, since my first kiss with Chris was on the sidewalk in front of The Joint. Get rid of the pain, my ass. Can you tell I'm still a little bit angry?

I've been reading some of *Breathless* every night for the last couple days. Marissa is right—it is really good. I can totally identify with Leesa, the main character. She's a college freshman, like me, and kind of shy and awkward—again like me. She's tall and loves to walk, too, despite a birth defect that makes her limp. She sounds like she's much prettier than me, but she doesn't realize how cute she is. Marissa would say that's just like me, too. Leesa's home life is totally messed up—way worse than mine, for sure. Her dad left when she was really young, and her mom won't go out of the house during the day, saying the sunlight hurts her skin because she was bitten by a one-fanged vampire, of all things. I bet you never heard of one-fanged vampires before. They're crippled versions of the real thing, and their bite passes on vampire weaknesses, like the sun-sensitivity thing, but not vampire powers. That sounds like a total bummer—if you're going to get bit, you should at least get the powers!

Anyhow, I guess I shouldn't complain too much about having parents whose biggest issue is all the fighting and bickering. It could be worse—much worse. Leesa does have a cool older brother who helped raise her, but he disappeared under mysterious circumstances, which might also involve vampires. Leesa is determined to find him. That's the driving force to the story.

I could go on and on about all the cool stuff in the book, but the part I've just *got* to talk about is the romance. Leesa meets this gorgeous guy named Rave. The chemistry between them is immediate—and powerful! But there are a couple of problems. Rave doesn't use phones or drive a car, or even ride in one. He won't use any sort of modern appliance, which makes him kind of hard to get a hold of, let alone get together with, especially since he doesn't live on campus. At first, Leesa thinks it's a religious thing, like the Amish, but she soon learns better. You see, Rave isn't human—and no, he's not a vampire, either. He's a volkaane. Volkaanes are supernatural vampire hunters. They look human, but they possess this magical inner fire they use to slay vampires. That's kind of cool right? To be dating a guy who can protect you from a vampire? Only problem is, the heat of his kiss could kill Leesa. And that's not so cool, no pun intended. Not cool at all.

Anyhow, despite all these obstacles, Leesa and Rave

fall in love. Some of their scenes together are so tender and passionate they almost make me change my mind about giving up on guys. But they make me sad, too. If Leesa and Rave can make things work despite all those challenges, how come I can't find a decent guy to be with? Maybe having a mother who was bitten by a vampire and a brother who disappears is less damaging than parents who fight and a boyfriend who cheated.

I have to remind myself it's only a book. And I don't know if Leesa and Rave will end up together or not. There's also a hot vampire who wants her. She wants Rave, of course, but she's hoping the vampire might be able to help her find her brother. And finding her brother is the most important thing in her life, so who knows what she's going to do. I can't wait to find out, though.

But there's no sense comparing my situation to Leesa and Rave's, because Rave isn't human. Human guys still suck. Maybe if I meet a volkaane, I'll give him a chance. Yeah, that's the ticket. I think I'll wait for that.

Marissa comes waltzing in through the door, so I close my book and sit up. She's been out with Andy tonight, and judging by the smile on her face and the bounce in her step, she had a good time. This is their fourth or fifth date since the frat party, and she's told me she's starting to really like him.

"Hey, Roomie," she says. She notices *Breathless* on my bed. "I bet you're loving that, huh?"

"Yeah, it's really good."

"I knew you would. Leesa kind of reminds me of you," Marissa says. "Really shy, but totally hot."

I blush and laugh at the same time. See, I knew she'd say something like that.

"I think she's way hotter," I say. "But thanks anyway.

How was your date?"

"Really fun. We went to the arcade. Played a couple of dance games—Andy's pretty good for a guy, but I kicked his butt." She does a couple of fancy dance moves in the center of the room to emphasize her point. "He got me back in the shoot-em ups, though. Then we went for some hot chocolate, and then back to his place to make out.

"Ewww, too much information!" I say, scrunching up my face. "Please, spare me the details."

Marissa laughs. "You sure? They're pretty hot."

I grin. "Yeah, believe me, I'm sure." I pick up *Breathless*. "I'm getting all the romance I need right here, thank you."

"Suit yourself." She turns and hangs her jacket in the closet. "Hey, I almost forgot," she says, turning back to me. "James gave us some tickets for open mic night at The Joint. Wanna come with us?"

I look at her like she's crazy. Sure, James seems like a nice guy and he's friends with Andy and all, but she knows I'm not interested in dating anyone. Not even close. Maybe she's trying to ease me back into the game.

But open mic night? What if Chris shows up? I really don't want to see the creep, let alone watch him play the piano.

"No, thanks," I say. "I'm really not ready for any dating, even if it's just a double date."

It's her turn to look at me like I'm crazy. "What double date? James gave us three passes. It'd be just you, me and Andy." She winks at me. "And we're not ready for a threesome yet, so it's definitely not a date. It'll just be a fun night out."

"I don't know," I say. "You-know-who could show

up. He likes open mic."

"Oh, yeah. I forgot about that," Marissa says. She thinks for a moment. "Tell you what, if he shows up, we'll all leave. The tickets are free, so it's not like we'd be losing anything if we have to split."

I'm still not sure. It would probably be fun, I know. But I'm still a little worried about running into Chris. But I can't let him dictate my life.

"Okay," I say. "I'm in. On one condition."

"Great," Marissa says. "What's the condition?"

I smile. "That you and Andy save all the mushy stuff until you're alone. I don't want to have to watch you two horn dogs going at each other."

Marissa laughs. "Fine by me," she says. "But it might be tough for Andy. I'm not sure he can keep his hands off me that long."

I laugh. "Tell him to try hard."

## CHAPTER 27

**I**'m getting ready for open mic night. Or trying to get ready, at least. I'm not having much luck deciding what to wear. I don't want to give anyone the idea I'm looking to hook up, but since I'm going with Andy and Marissa, I can't go as a total slob, either. Marissa suggested my leggings and boots with a sweater or something, but that's way too much of a "look at me" outfit. I've settled on a pair of semi-dressy jeans—one of my looser pairs—but haven't figured out my top yet. All my T-shirts seem too casual.

I look over at Marissa. She's having no trouble at all, but that's because it's a date with her boyfriend. So of course she wants to look hot. She's already dressed and is putting on her makeup. She's wearing a pair of tight jeans and black leather boots with three inch heels. The jeans are stylishly faded across the front of her thighs. Her dark blue pullover shirt is cut so that it's casual and sexy at same time. It's loose off one shoulder at the top and slightly baggy at the bottom, but cut more tightly around her chest. And just to make sure no one misses her curves, three narrow light blue stripes stretch horizontally across her chest. I have to admit, she certainly does have a sexy little figure. And she knows how to work it, too.

I go back to rummaging through my closet, finally settling on a collarless burnt orange shirt with a two button neck. I pull it on over my head and check myself out in the mirror. Casual enough, but dressier than a T-shirt. So far, so good. Now, what to do with my hair?

It's down right now, but no way am I going to leave it that way. Guys like long hair way too much. I gather it in my hand and hold it atop my head like it's in a bun, but with my collarless shirt, that exposes way too much neck. Guys like necks, too. I think they must have vampire blood in them. So no bun, either.

I twist my hair into a loose braid and fasten it at the bottom with a plain rubber band. Much better—sloppy but contained. I flip the braid over the front of my left shoulder. Perfect!

Turning from the mirror, I see Marissa watching me. She's got a big grin on her face.

"Trying not to look too hot, huh?" she says.

I smile sheepishly. This whole thing is ironic, because I've never thought I was all that cute, but here I am worrying about it, in an ass-backwards way, yet. See what you've done to me, Chris?

"Most of us work hard trying to look good," Marissa says, shaking her head. "You work harder not to. Must be a nice problem to have." She's still smiling, so I know she's only teasing.

"I just don't want anyone getting the wrong idea," I say.

"Maybe you should hang an 'off limits' sign around

your neck," Marissa suggests.

I rub my chin, like I'm considering the idea. "That's a great idea. Maybe I can get a fake engagement ring somewhere, too. To keep away any guys who can't read."

"Good thinking. And just to be sure, we can put some barbed wire around our table."

We're both laughing now.

Andy steps in through the open door. "What's got you two laughing so hard?" he asks.

Marissa crosses to him and gives him a quick peck on the mouth.

"We're figuring out ways to keep guys away from Heather," she says.

"So far, we've come up with an engagement ring, an off limits sign and barbed wire," I say. "But I'm open to suggestions."

"Heck," Andy says, grinning. "Just hire some old guy with a shotgun to sit next to you. Nothing keeps guys away better than an angry father with a double barrel, trust me."

We all laugh.

"You got some experience with that, frat boy?" Marissa asks teasingly.

"I'll never tell," Andy replies.

Marissa snuggles against him and rubs her hand seductively over his stomach. "You sure about that?" she asks. "I bet I can get it out of you," she adds as she rubs him again, a little bit lower this time.

"Hey! None of that," I say. "Remember our agreement."

Marissa laughs and steps away from him. Andy looks from Marissa to me and then back to Marissa.

"What agreement?" he asks.

"Heather said she would only go to open mic if I promised that you and I would save any mushy stuff for later," Marissa explains. She looks at me and smiles. "But you didn't say anything about sex stuff."

"I didn't think I needed to," I say, shaking my head. "You're such a perv."

"I'm not a perv," Marissa says. "I just have healthy appetites."

Andy laughs. "She just can't keep her hands off me, that's all."

"That's what she said about you," I say, smiling now. "But either way, no more of that stuff till you guys are alone... got it?"

"Yes, mother," Marissa says. "I promise we'll behave ourselves."

"So, you girls ready to go?" Andy asks. "You both look great, by the way." He immediately corrects himself. "I mean, you look great, Marissa. Totally hot." He smiles at me. "Heather, you look just okay."

"Nice save, Andy," I say. "That's exactly the look I was going for—just okay." I grab my coat from the closet. "So I guess I'm ready."

Marissa gets her coat and the three of us head out the door to the elevator.

There's a short line in front of The Joint, so even though we've got passes, we have to wait outside a few moments while the less lucky kids pay the small cover charge. Standing there, I can feel my stomach beginning to get a little nervous. I haven't been here since that night with

Chris, and there's always a chance he could be inside. I hate to admit it, but a small part of me still wants to see him. But a much bigger piece of me hopes I never have to look at his cheating face again. I'm glad Marissa promised we'd all leave if he's here. I wouldn't really make her and Andy leave—that wouldn't really be fair—but her promise gives me the freedom to scoot if I need to.

When we get to the front of the line, I see a familiar face seated on a stool beside the door, collecting the cover charges and passes.

It's James, from the frat party. Suddenly the pieces all fit. No wonder he knew about me and Chris and the piano playing—he'd been working that night. And now I know why Marissa and Andy were so anxious for me to join them tonight, and why James had free passes. Mixed metaphors aside, I can smell a fix-up when I see one. I glance at Marissa, intent on giving her the evil eye, but she's smiling at me all sweet and innocent like. All I can manage is to shake my head in resignation. Well played, roomie.

I have to admit, James does look good in his pale blue long-sleeve shirt. I think it's the rolled up sleeves that do it, making him look smart and casual, rather than stuffy. His forearms are pretty muscular, and I find myself wishing I could see a little more of his arms.

"There must be some mistake here," James says playfully. "What are two such lovely ladies doing with this loser?"

Andy grins and holds his fist out for a fist bump. "Jealousy does not become you, my friend," he says.

"Thanks for the passes, James," Marissa says.

"No problem," James says.

He turns to me and smiles. "Hi, Heather. It's nice to see you again."

"You, too," is about all I can manage to say.

"I hope tonight is more fun for you than our frat party was," James says.

"It really wasn't so bad," I say. I notice that somehow my hand has made it to my hair and is playing with the end of my braid, so I force my hand back to my side. "I'm sure tonight will be fun, though."

Andy and James exchange another fist bump and then we step through the doorway.

Inside, the place is about half full. There's one group of seven or eight very loud guys near the front. A couple of them are really big—jocks from the football team, most likely. Thankfully, the hostess guides us to a table on the other side of the room, about half way back. If the behavior of the guys up front is any indication of how they'll behave during the performances, I feel sorry for anyone who gets up on stage and is not *really* good. I can't even play for my friends—how someone will manage to perform with those guys right in front of them is beyond me. We're sitting far enough away that their noise is merely annoying, but not overly bothersome. Not yet, anyhow. I hope they'll quiet down a bit during the show, though. Either that, or I hope they have good bouncers here. I wonder if James is a bouncer. He's tall and pretty well built, but he doesn't really look like the bouncer type.

The hostess gives us each a menu and skitters away to seat the next party. On the way to our table, I took a quick scan of the place looking for Chris, but now that we're sitting, I do a more careful check. My heart momentarily skips a beat when I spot a brown fedora across the room, but the guy is blond and way too short to be Chris. There's no sign of him, and I feel myself relax a bit. I look over at Marissa and see that she's watching me.

"So far, so good, huh?" she says. "No sign of he-who-shall-not-be named?"

Marissa has taken to using the Harry Potter Voldemort reference when referring to Chris. Hearing his name doesn't really upset me anymore, but I haven't disabused her of the notion. Who knows, it might come in handy one of these days if I need to get out of doing something.

I shake my head. "Nope. He's not here. Let's hope it stays that way."

"Great," Marissa says. "So it's safe to order some food? I'm hungry."

"Me, too," Andy says.

I pick up my menu and smile. "Well, what are you waiting for then?"

I give the menu only a cursory glance. I don't feel like a hamburger, and the chicken sandwich was pretty tasty last time, so my choice is easy. Marissa and Andy put their menus down a few moments after I do, and less than a minute later, a waiter arrives at our table.

"What can I get you guys?" he asks.

I order my chicken sandwich and a diet cola, while Andy and Marissa both opt for BuzzBurgers. Marissa asks for a lemonade and Andy orders a soda. We also order a jumbo basket of fries we'll all share.

"Coming right up," the waiter says as he finishes

scribbling the order on his pad.

"You two probably think you're so smart," I say after he spins away from the table and heads toward the kitchen.

Marissa gives me that innocent look again. "I'm sure I don't know what you mean, Heather," she says, smiling sweetly.

"Yeah, I'm sure," I say. I shake my head. "I should have known when you said you had three passes and not four. Was James behind all this?"

Andy and Marissa exchange a glance.

"Actually, he did give me four passes," Andy says.

"I knew you wouldn't go with anyone," Marissa says, "so I figured it'd be easier if I just told you we only had three tickets. That way you wouldn't worry about us setting you up with someone."

For a moment, I'm worried that's exactly what they've done, and that some friend of Andy's is going to appear with the fourth pass and join us at our table. My concern must show on my face, because Marissa quickly reassures me.

"Don't worry, Heather," she says. "We didn't give the extra pass to anybody. It's just the three of us."

I'm glad to hear that. And I'm also glad to hear that James wasn't behind this whole thing. But I still think there's more to it than Marissa is admitting.

"So my name never came up when James gave you the tickets?" I ask Andy.

Andy looks like he doesn't really want to be part of this conversation. He glances at Marissa. "Well, he might have mentioned something about bringing Marissa and her friend," he says.

I can tell there's more. "And?" I ask.

"James said he thought you could use some fun, that's all. So he suggested we all come to open mic night."

I look at Marissa. "And you knew James worked here, of course."

"Well, yeah. But that's just it, Heather—he's working. So it's not like it's a date or anything."

"And there's no plan for the four of us to get together after the show?" I ask.

Marissa does a crossing her heart gesture with her fingers. "No, I promise," she says. "Nothing at all."

I look at Andy for confirmation.

"No plans," he says. "James helps with the cleanup after they close. We'll be long gone before he's done."

"Okay," I say. "You guys are off the hook...for now, anyhow."

I'm glad to hear there are no ulterior motives behind our night out, but I'm surprised to find myself a little disappointed this wasn't more of a setup. I'm certainly not going to tell them that, though. Especially since I don't quite understand it myself.

The arrival of our food keeps me from having to think about it any further.

## CHAPTER 28

My chicken sandwich is even better than I remember—the cook's spicy Dijon sauce is totally delicious. The chunky fries are tasty, too. Marissa and Andy seem to be enjoying their Buzzburgers as well.

Our waiter begins clearing our plates away almost as soon as we finish eating. I think we're getting special service, which is nice, because the MC is making his way toward the stage. It's the same guy as last time.

James materializes at our table, standing behind Andy.

"Have fun, guys," he says, before heading back toward the door, where his stool is now just inside the doorway.

James seemed to be talking to all three of us, but I have the feeling his comment was really directed at me. And why not? He's probably seen Andy and Marissa together enough to know they'll be having a good time regardless of the performers. I'm the one who admitted to not having much fun at the frat party.

The MC's welcome speech is basically the same as the last time, as is his introduction of the first guest, Tony

Phillips. The crowd cheers as Phillips makes his way to the stage with his guitar. Clearly, there are plenty of regulars here who know what song Phillips is going to sing.

Sure enough, he launches into his traditional opening number, his custom written rendition of "I Love The Joint." He's barely into the song before a number of people are singing along with him. I find myself humming to the melody.

Apparently, the Gaga guy from last time isn't here tonight, because when Phillips finishes to a loud ovation, the MC is back on stage asking who wants to be next. For a moment, nobody moves, but then an older guy—forties maybe—in a black button shirt and dark blue jeans makes his way toward the stage. His curly black hair is flecked with gray and reaches to his shoulders. I wonder if he works on campus—he looks like he could be a professor— or if he's just someone who lives near campus and has somehow managed to discover The Joint's open mic night. Either way, he's prepared, because he's carrying a large music player up to the stage with him.

He takes a minute to plug in and set up the player before grabbing the old guitar from the back of the stage. He hooks the strap over his shoulder and strums the guitar a few times.

"This old girl isn't quite enough to do justice to the song I want to play for you," he says. He takes a moment to twist a couple of the keys, tuning the guitar, and then plays a few more chords. Apparently, he's satisfied now, because he moves closer to the microphone.

"Back in the day," he says, "I used to have a band behind me." He reaches over and pats the top of the music player. "Tonight, this thing will have to do."

He strums another couple of chords. "Any of you kids ever hear of something called…" he pauses for effect, and then shouts: "rock and roll?"

Some boisterous cheers erupt from the audience. He flips a switch on the music player and launches into a rousing rendition of Springsteen's "Born to Run." This guy is totally talented—his old band must have really rocked. By the time he's done, the crowd is clapping and singing along, and a dozen or so kids are dancing in any open spaces they can find. Rock and roll never dies… or even gets old. Just ask my dad.

The MC is heading toward the stage, but the old guy is not finished.

"You folks want another one?" he screams into the microphone.

The response is immediate and overwhelming. Shouts of "Yeah!" and "Encore" fill the room. The MC backs away. He knows a good thing when he hears it.

The singer leans the guitar back against the wall and fiddles with his music player for a moment. He grabs the microphone out of its stand and begins singing "Satisfaction," mimicking Mick Jagger's antic moves as he bounces across the stage. This performance is even better than his "Born to Run."

He leaves the stage to thunderous applause, a huge smile on his sweat-soaked face. He's clearly thrilled to have relived some piece of his past. I wonder who's going to have the guts to go on after him. He'll be a hard act to follow.

Some groans from the back of the room give me my

first clue. I turn and see a familiar sight. It's the comedian in the loud suit who bombed so badly the last time I was here. The groans grow louder as he nears the stage. Obviously, a lot of people here have heard him before—and are not all that anxious to hear him again.

I've got to give the guy credit. He doesn't seem to let the catcalls and groans bother him at all. He's either got the thickest skin in the world, or he just figures the derision is in some twisted way an approval of his act. His jokes are all new, but are equally as dumb as the last time. I wonder if he writes this stuff himself or gets it from some website—stupidjokes.com, maybe.

The big guys up front heckle him mercilessly after every punch line. It's mean and obnoxious and most of their comments are only funny to their table. I notice James is watching them closely from his perch by the door. Finally, the biggest guy, a brute with shoulders as wide as an SUV, yells something really crude, something not fit even for this very liberal college crowd. James strides quickly over to the table. He leans over and says something into the guy's ear. The guy starts to stand, but James pushes his hand down on the brute's shoulder, forcing him back into his chair.

Andy is immediately on his feet, ready to go to his frat brother's aid, and I see two waiters also beginning to converge on the table. I'm afraid we're about to have an all out brawl and that James is going to get himself pummeled by the giant. But James leans down again, his hand still on the guy's shoulder, and says something else. The brute nods vigorously and throws his hands up in a gesture of surrender. I don't know how James did it, or what he said, but he definitely got that guy's attention. I watch and see the guy talking to his buddies, who all nod back at him. Finally, James lets go of his shoulder. Everyone at the table gets up and meekly leaves the room.

As soon as they're gone, the audience erupts into applause almost as loud as the rock and roll guy got. James smiles and waits for the clapping to subside, then nods to the guy on stage to continue his act. The would be comedian picks up where he left off without missing a beat as James melts back into the dimness at the side of the room.

Finally, the guy is done. He smiles as he receives a smattering of polite applause. I'm pretty sure the applause is mostly in sympathy for how he was treated by the now vacant table. Catcalls and groans are apparently fair game, but meanness is not, and those guys had gone way over the line. Whatever the reason, the guy is clearly pleased by the reaction.

Two girls and one guy are heading quickly toward the stage from different directions, each eager to be the one to follow that act. The guy does the gentlemanly thing and backs off when he sees the two girls also making for the stage, leaving them to figure out who goes next. One is tall and dark-haired, with bright red lipstick and a full sleeve of colorful tattoos covering her right arm. The other is much shorter, blond and fair, wearing a pretty blue and orange dress. If they end up fighting for the spot, my money is definitely on tattoo girl.

The two of them converse for a moment, and then the blonde sits at the piano while tattoo girl grabs the guitar. Apparently, they know at least one common song and are going to play together. Good for them. Make love, not war.

I've been so busy watching them I don't notice James making his way to our table. Suddenly, I realize he's standing behind the empty chair next to me.

"Ten minute break," he says. "You guys mind if I take a load off for a few?"

"Sure, have a seat," Andy says.

James is polite enough to look at me to see if it's okay. He's been so easygoing about everything, how can I say no? Besides, it's only ten minutes, and it's not like he's hitting on me or anything. He just wants to take his break with some friends, right?

I nod my okay, so he pulls out the chair and sits.

"Good job with those jerks," Andy says. "Very smooth."

James shrugs. "It was time for them to leave." He says it like it's no big deal, but that's not how it looked from back here.

"I thought I was going to have to bail your ass out," Andy says. "But you obviously had things well in hand."

"What did you say to that guy to make him calm down like that?" I ask. "He was huge."

"I just told him this is a friendly place and we don't tolerate rude behavior."

"No way," Marissa says. "He bought that?"

"I don't get it either," I say. "He looked like he wanted to kill you."

James smiles. "It wasn't so much what I said as how I said it. My brother's in Special Forces. He taught me a few tricks." He puts his hand lightly on my shoulder.

A tingling sensation shoots through me, like a weak electric current. What the heck is that about? Did I really just feel that? Was it a surge of desire—or of fear? I don't have a clue. I'm pretty sure I don't want to know, anyhow.

"There's bundle of nerve endings right here," James explains. "Squeezing them is *very* painful, and I had a tight grip on his. I told him if I wanted to I could break his shoulder, and his coach wouldn't be very happy about that." He smiles again and removes his hand. "I couldn't break it, of course, at least not by squeezing, but I'm sure it hurt enough so he believed I could."

Well, so much for that desire-fear thing. Whatever I felt was just his fingers triggering that bunch of nerve endings—I think.

"Perception is reality," Andy says.

"Hey, smart boy," Marissa says, giving Andy's forearm a playful squeeze. "That's very deep. Where'd you learn that?"

"Oh, it's just something I picked up in one of my psych classes," Andy says. "If you study hard, sweetheart, and do all your homework, one day maybe you'll be as smart as me."

Marissa laughs and bats her eyelashes at him. "A girl can only dream," she says.

James and I shake our heads at the two of them and laugh.

The girls on stage have worked out whatever they needed to work out, because the blonde at the piano begins to play. A moment later, tattoo girl joins in with her guitar, and I immediately recognize Lady Antebellum's "Need You Now." The blonde starts singing first, so I guess tattoo girl will do the guy part. They both have pretty good voices, but it's still a bit disconcerting watching two women sing that song. But they really are good, and the crowd gives them a nice round of applause.

"Did anyone else find that a tad strange," Andy asks. "Or is it just me?"

"What's the matter?" Marissa asks, grinning. "Aren't you into the girl-girl thing?"

"I'm not sure how to answer that," Andy says, returning her grin. "Not in mixed company, anyhow."

I decide to come to Andy's defense, not that he needs it. "I thought it was a bit weird at first, too" I say. "But they both have really good voices, so I liked it."

James slides his chair back and stands up. "I'd love to hear how this discussion ends," he says, smiling, "but I've got to get back to work. Have fun, guys."

"Try not to work too hard," Andy says.

We listen to a bunch more acts, some good, some not so good, before I decide to it's time to bring the night to an end. I've been having fun, but I want Marissa and Andy to have some alone time. They deserve a reward for keeping any romantic stuff between them to a bare minimum for more than two hours.

"This has been great, guys," I say, "but I think I'm ready to call it a night. I'm getting kind of tired."

"You sure?" Marissa asks.

I'm pretty sure she knows what I'm thinking. And I'm also pretty sure she can't wait to be alone with Andy, but she's putting me above her desires. She's such a good friend.

"Yeah," I say. "You guys can stay, though. I'll be

okay."

"No, we'll walk you home," Andy says. He looks at Marissa and grins. "I'm sure Marissa and I will come up with something to do afterwards."

"Ha! Don't get your hopes up, frat boy," Marissa says. But from the smile on her face and the way she's circled her hands around behind the crook of his elbow, I'm pretty sure Andy doesn't have to worry about his hopes being unduly high.

We stop for a quick chat with James on the way out.

"Thanks for the passes, bro," Andy says.

"Yeah, thank you," I say. "It was a lot of fun."

"I'm glad you all enjoyed it," James says. "Come anytime."

I'm not sure, but I think he was looking at me when he said that last part.

## CHAPTER 29

It's Wednesday afternoon, and I'm sitting in algebra, my final class of the holiday-shortened week. I'm definitely not enjoying it, but that's nothing new. Tomorrow is Thanksgiving, and I thought about using the holiday as an excuse to skip out on this class, but math is hard enough without missing any time. Judging by the number of empty seats, though, not all my classmates are as conscientious. Either that, or math is coming easier to them and they're not worried about missing one class.

So here I am, bored out of my skull but trying to pay attention as the professor scribbles X's and Y's and other symbols on the whiteboard. Only twenty more minutes and class will be over. Then it's back to the dorm to throw some stuff together for the long weekend. Mom's going to pick me up at four o'clock.

The break from classes will be nice, and it's always good to see Sam, but four days at home is one or two more than I'd really like. The freedom and the absence of bickering here at school have definitely weakened my tolerance for mom and dad's arguing. I've been home for dinner four or five times since I had my friends over, but I only stayed overnight once. Dad drove me back to school on his way to work the next morning. I spent the evening taking Sam for a long walk and studying, so it wasn't too bad. But that was only one night, not four in a row.

Mom asked if I wanted to bring my boyfriend home for Thanksgiving dinner. I told her he was never really a boyfriend and that we weren't seeing each other anymore. I don't discuss a lot of personal stuff with my folks, for obvious reasons, and I'm certainly not going to go into the whole Chris debacle with them, even if I wasn't working so hard at trying to put it behind me.

Mom was disappointed—she worries about my lack of boyfriends. I think she's afraid there's something wrong with me. Well, guess what, mom? There is something wrong with your daughter—it's called poor parental role modeling!

She also told me I could invite any of my friends, which would have been really nice, but they all have family dinners of their own to go to. At least Aunt Barbara and my three cousins will be joining us for Thanksgiving. Cousin Jamie is only a year younger than me, and we get along really well. Plus, mom and dad usually behave a little better when we have company.

The rest of the weekend I'm on my own, I'm afraid. Geesh, I haven't even left for home yet, and I'm already looking forward to coming back to school on Sunday. How sad—or sick—is that?

Finally, the professor puts his marker down and finishes class by giving us our homework assignment. I'm out the door before his "Have a nice Thanksgiving" is done echoing off the walls.

Back at the dorm, I begin packing for my long weekend. Marissa's last class ended an hour earlier than mine, so she's already left for home. We said our goodbyes at lunch. I'm going to miss her. A lot. Most of the girls on my floor have gone already, so it's quieter than usual. I can hear music from the other end of the hall, but it's too faint for me to recognize the song. I wonder if anyone in the dorm isn't going home, because it's too far or too expensive or something. Since it's a state school, most of the kids live within easy distance, but there are some from other parts of the country. For some reason, I think about James. He told me he hates his home town, so I wonder if that means he doesn't even go home for the holidays. From what he's hinted about his father, I wouldn't be surprised if James remains on campus. Maybe I should have invited *him* to Thanksgiving dinner.

I still have plenty of clothes at my house, especially winter stuff, so I don't need to bring any with me. I just have to gather my personal stuff, a few other odds and ends, and some of my books. The books will make a great excuse to disappear into my room whenever I feel the need. What parent could argue with a child who wants to study?

I pull my guitar case out of the closet—no way am I going to brave four days at home without my guitar—and I'm ready to roll. With so many kids already gone, I think I'll be able to make it out of the dorm without seeing anyone I know. One of these days, I'm going to have to let Katie and Beth, at least, know that I play. Maybe next semester.

Just to be safe, I leave my guitar propped against the

wall inside my door while I cross the hall and push the button to summon the elevator. No sense standing there with my guitar case for anyone to see while I wait for the elevator to arrive.

The bell dings and I quickly grab my guitar and lock my door. I have plenty of time to step into the elevator before the door slides closed. Outside, mom is pulling to the curb in front of my dorm just as I exit the building, so I don't have to wait at all. Sam is in the back seat, bouncing around with the kind of excitement only a dog can manage. I'm happy to see him, too, even if I'm not bouncing around quite so much. I throw my stuff into the rear cargo area, out of his reach, then open the back door and give Sam a quick kiss and a chest rub. Finally, I climb into the front seat beside my mom.

"Hi, sweetheart," she says, leaning over to give me a kiss on the cheek. "It's going to be so nice to have you home for a couple of days. Your father and I have missed you."

I return her kiss. It is good to see her. Both my folks—especially mom—are usually okay to be with alone. It's only when they're together that they get on my nerves so badly.

"Yeah, it'll be nice," I say. "I've really been looking forward to getting a break from classes. It'll be fun to see Aunt Barbara and Jamie, too."

Mom smiles at me and starts the car. Away we go, to what I hope will be a very uneventful holiday weekend.

## CHAPTER 30

I get my wish—Thanksgiving weekend passes without much trouble at all. Dinner was delicious. Dad fried a twenty pound turkey out in the back yard, while mom and Aunt Barbara whipped up a bunch of tasty side dishes in the kitchen, including a pumpkin pie mom made from scratch that was totally awesome. With Dad out back for most of the day and mom inside, there wasn't much opportunity for them to fight. My cousins and I shuttled back and forth from hanging with my dad outside to visiting with mom and Aunt Barbara inside while they cooked.

Mom and dad have one big blow-up on Saturday afternoon. It starts with dad complaining about eating leftovers again—uh, Dad, *everybody* eats leftovers on Thanksgiving weekend—and escalates from there. I grab Sam and take him for a two hour walk. By the time we get back, mom is watching television in the living room and dad is busy in his den. I join mom, who's watching some old movie with Barbara Streisand and Kris Kristofferson. I guess he was a pretty good country music singer back in the day, but that was way before my time. The movie's got some good singing in it, so I hang around and watch for awhile.

Sunday is pretty uneventful, by mom and dad's standard, anyhow, and by mid-afternoon, dad is dropping me off in front of my dorm. All in all, it wasn't a bad weekend, not by any stretch.

I'm glad to be back, though. It's only for three weeks this time, and then it will be Christmas break. That two week break promises to be much more of a challenge than Thanksgiving, but I'm not going to worry about it now. Besides, I've survived seventeen Christmases. I'm sure can handle another one.

The door to my room is part way open, so I know Marissa has beaten me back. I hear Taylor Swift singing "Last Christmas" through the doorway as I cross the hall. I guess Marissa is thinking about Christmas break already, too, although probably not in the same way I am. "Last Christmas" is actually pretty sad for a holiday song, but Taylor makes it sound beautiful. I suppose I should count my blessings that Chris broke my heart at Halloween instead of Christmas. That would have made Christmas really tough to handle—and maybe messed up my next few Christmases as well.

My hands are full, so I push the door open with my shoulder and walk in. Beth is here, sitting on Marissa's desk chair. Marissa is perched comfortably on her bed. I guess they've been catching up on their weekends.

"Hey, I didn't know you played guitar," Beth says, her eyes fixed on my guitar case as I walk in.

Busted! I guess it had to happen sometime. I drop my stuff onto my bed and shove the case into the closet. I'm not quite ready to cop to my playing yet.

"I don't, really," I say. "But I want to learn."

"All that *Guitar Hero* has you fired up, huh?" Beth says.

"Yeah, something like that, I guess," I say.

I see Marissa roll her eyes at me, but she doesn't say anything about it, for which I'm grateful.

"So, Roomie," she says instead. "How was your weekend?"

And with that, the three of us launch into a long discussion of our Thanksgiving weekends. Katie joins us a little while later. It's like we never left.


The first two weeks back fly by, and then it's time for final exams. Whoopie!

Finals are way worse than midterms. Not only is there twice as much material to study and try to remember, but the exams count as a bigger portion of the final grade. So the pressure is that much greater. Glassy stares are the norm out in the hallway, and if I had the time, I'd recycle the piles of energy drink cans that keep the trash bin outside the dorm overflowing. I could make a nice little chunk of cash from them, I bet. I could probably make some decent money just from the cans Marissa and I are going through.

But, alas, there's no time for anything but studying, eating and sleeping—and little enough for the latter two. I can't believe I have to go through this hell seven more times before I graduate. I sure hope it gets easier with experience.

I do most of my studying in my room, but I head over

to the library for an hour or two every day, just for a break in the routine. It's also a good place to remind myself that lots of kids are even more stressed about finals than I am. Some look like they haven't slept—or showered—in days.

I also make sure I take a couple of short walks every day, to clear my head and stretch my muscles. I usually drag Marissa, Katie or Beth with me, but sometimes I go alone. I don't go far, just wander about the area around the dorm. I'd love to go the park, but that's a longer walk than I have time for. The weather's been cold, but luckily it's been clear. I don't know what I'd do if we had a rainy week, or worse. The walk breaks are the only thing keeping me sane, I think. That and my guitar, which I play for a little while every night, studying be damned. Marissa doesn't mind—if she's here when I play, she takes a break from her studying to listen. A couple times, she's gotten up and danced to the music.

Thursday afternoon. Three finals down and only one to go, tomorrow morning. Psychology. That one shouldn't be too bad, except I haven't done much studying for it yet, because I had my algebra exam this morning and I had to give that one most of my attention. I stayed up until almost four o'clock studying for it. The test was a beast, but I think I did okay. I might eek out a B for the semester, which would be great. Better than great. If I only get a C, that's okay, too. It's math, after all.

I wolf down a peanut butter and jelly sandwich and decide to take a walk before I hit my psych books. I throw on a pair of gray sweatpants and a heavy, dark red hoodie. I've got two shirts on under the hoodie, one long sleeve and one short, so I'll be plenty warm. I tuck my hair up under a brown knit cap and I'm ready to go. No fashion plate, for sure, but who cares? It's finals week. And who do I need to impress, anyhow?

The cold air hits me as soon as I step out of the dorm. I shove my hands into my sweatshirt pockets and make a beeline for the sunny side of the street. Once I get my blood flowing, I'll be fine.

I've gone barely a block when I hear a familiar voice behind me. It's Andy.

"Hey, Heather," he calls.

I turn and see Andy and James coming up behind me. Andy's bundled up in a heavy gray State sweatshirt and jeans, with a red baseball cap on his head. James is also wearing jeans, with a brown leather bomber jacket. His head is bare.

"Hi, Andy," I say. "Hi, James."

"Hi, Heather," James says. "How are you enjoying your first finals week?"

James looks even more tired than I feel. A stubble of blonde whiskers covers his chin and his eyes are red. His smile is alive and friendly, though.

"Ugggh," I say. "Don't ask. I'm bushed. I haven't had more than a couple hours sleep any night this week. Thank god I've only got one final to go."

"You should try studying for finals *and* working at the same time," James says. "No fun, believe me."

"You've been working at The Joint this week?" I ask, amazed. No wonder he looks so tired. "Wouldn't they let you off for finals?"

"Almost all the employees are students," James says.

"If they let us off, they'd have to shut the place down for the week. At least they work with us in terms of our schedules. I've been helping out waiting tables, too, covering for some of the kids who have insane exam schedules."

"I can't even imagine having to work this week," I say. "You definitely have my sympathy. And my admiration."

"We're heading to The Joint to get something to eat," Andy says. "Wanna join us?"

I shake my head. "No thanks. I just had a PB&J. I'm just taking a short break before I go back and hit the books some more."

"Good luck with your last test," James says. "And have a great Christmas."

"Thanks," I say. "You, too. Are you going home for break?"

"No, I'm staying here," he says. "I can pick up some more extra shifts at The Joint, since a couple of the waiters will be gone. I can always use the extra money."

I start to make a sympathetic remark, but catch myself, remembering what he told me about his father.

"That's cool," I say instead.

"If you get bored over vacation, come on out to The Joint," James says. "I'll be working pretty much every night. I'll get you the employee discount for dinner."

"We'll see," I say, ever the cautious girl. "I'd better head back. Enjoy your lunch. See you both next year."

The next morning, I walk out of my psych final with a big smile on my face. I'm pretty sure I aced the thing, so that's a great way to end my first semester of college. Now all I have to do is pack some stuff and wait for dad to pick me up. It's been a pretty eventful four months, that's for sure.

I wonder what spring semester will have in store for me....

# CHAPTER 31

"Spring semester" is a total misnomer, at least for right now. We don't get much snow here, but we had a couple of inches two days before school started. The roads and sidewalks are mostly clear, but there's still some snow blanketing the lawns, especially in the shaded areas, and lots more piled in long, rapidly blackening heaps along the curbs and at the edges of the parking lots. Nothing about the campus right now is remotely Spring-like.

But it's still good to be back.

My schedule for this semester isn't too much different from last semester. I have three required classes: English Literature, Introduction to Biology, and Algebra II— thankfully, that's the last math class I'll ever have to take! For electives, I have Introduction to Sociology and Animal Psychology. This semester will probably be a lot tougher than the last one, because I have five full-size courses instead of four. I don't have anything as fun and easy as the vampire class—and believe me, I looked for something. On the plus side, I won't have to worry about seeing Chris in class this term. If he shows up in one of my freshman level courses, I'll know he's stalking me.

I'm pretty much over all the surface hurt—the crying, the anger, the wondering how he could do that to me—but I have no idea how deep the scars might go. I was already a very cautious girl before him, but now I don't know how I'll ever really trust a guy again. But maybe that's okay. Not every girl needs to be with a guy, does she? If I never have another boyfriend, then I'll never have to worry about ending up in a relationship like my parents.

It's not like I'll be a hermit. I've got great girlfriends to do things with. I can still have lots of fun—the Halloween party and open mic night, as well as other things I did with my friends, proved that. Maybe somewhere down the line I'll find a guy friend—not a boyfriend, just a guy to be friends with, to get a little male energy in my life without having to worry about all the crap that goes with being in a relationship. Hey, a girl can dream, right?

The first two weeks of spring semester are fairly easy, as the professors ease us back into the academic grind. And that's just fine with me. With minimal homework and no tests to study for, there's plenty of time for fun. The only glitch in the whole thing is really just a selfish one on my part. Katie is still seeing Grant, and Marissa and Andy are doing great, so Katie and Marissa are not quite as available to play as they would be in my perfect world. But I certainly don't begrudge them their happiness, not at all. I still hang out with them plenty. Beth and I have been playing a lot of *Guitar Hero* and stuff, but I still haven't been able to convince her to hike in the park with me, even with the snow long gone. She's just not into nature stuff—

or exercise, for that matter—so if Marissa and Katie are busy with their guys, I end up going alone. Which is okay, because it's kind of peaceful.

Since I'm pretty sure I'm never going to date again, I'm trying to do everything I can to get even closer to my girlfriends. And that has led me to a really big decision—a monumental decision, for me, anyhow. I've decided to tell Katie and Beth that I play guitar, and even bolder, I'm going to play for them. And sing, too. Marissa is all for it, but I'm pretty nervous. Still, I'm determined to open up to them as much as I can. My music is an important part of me, and I want to share it with them. That's how you get close to people, right? By letting them into the more private aspects of your life. So that's what I'm going to do. Tonight's the night.

"So, what's the big news, Heather?" Beth asks.

I asked Beth and Heather to keep tonight free, and to come by my room at seven o'clock. I've haven't told them why, in case I chicken out. But I don't think Marissa will let me back out now even if I want to. She says I'm good enough to play for anyone, and that she's tired of having to keep my guitar playing a secret from our friends.

So here we are, gathered in my room. Marissa is sitting on her bed. Katie is next to her, and Beth has just settled onto one of the chairs. I'm too nervous to sit, so I'm standing and pacing. My guitar case is lying on my bed.

"I wanted to share something with you guys," I say. "You'll probably think it's no big deal, but it is to me, I promise. Very few people know about it."

I can tell by the look on their faces they are totally puzzled.

"Whatever it is, you can trust us, Heather," Katie says.

"Yeah," Beth says. "Unless you're going to tell us you've been having sex behind our backs." She grins. "I'm not sure I can forgive you if you've been holding out on something like that."

"Don't worry," I say, chuckling. "It's nothing *that* big, believe me."

I'm feeling a bit embarrassed that I'm making such a production out of this, so I cross to my bed and open my guitar case. Gingerly, I lift out my guitar.

"It's about this," I say. "My guitar is really important to me, but I've been keeping it a secret. Marissa is the only one who's heard me play." I sit down on my chair, with my guitar on my lap. "I want to share it with you guys, too. Because you're my friends."

"Cool," Katie says.

Beth still looks confused. "I don't understand what the big deal is," she says. "You've only had that thing a month or so, right?"

Marissa starts to laugh, but she covers her mouth with her hand. It's my show, and she's going to let me proceed however I want to.

"Well, not exactly," I say. I begin strumming the strings.

I spent quite awhile wrestling with what song to begin with. I finally decided to go with one I'm least likely to screw up, no matter how nervous I am. It's one of the first songs I learned, one that I've played so often I could probably do it in my sleep. It's a Taylor Swift song, of course. I'm going to play "Tim McGraw."

I don't think I could have done this one a month or two ago. The words of wistful love would have hurt too much after Chris. But like I said, I'm mostly over that now.

My fingers quickly fall into the familiar patterns. For a minute or two, I just play, eyes closed to block out my audience. It's just me and my guitar, the way it always is—and the music. Finally, I begin singing.

I don't open my eyes until I'm done. My three friends are smiling at me, big time.

"Wow, that was really good, Heather," Katie says.

"Yeah," Beth says, "and sooo not the performance of someone who has only played guitar for a month."

"Uh, yeah, about that," I say. "I may have fibbed just a little bit there."

I tell them how I've been playing for years, but had never played for anyone, not even my mom and dad, until I played for Marissa last semester. I open up about how important my guitar is to me, and how I use it to escape when things get too messed up at home, or when I'm down about something else. I explain why I decided to play for them, how I wanted us to be even closer than we already are. I finish by asking them not to tell anyone else about my playing. I'm not ready for that yet.

"I'm not even allowed to tell Andy," Marissa tells them. "And I tell him everything." She grins. "Well, almost everything."

Katie comes over and gives me a big hug. "I, for one, am very touched by your sharing this," she says.

"Me, too," Beth says. "And now I know why you rock *Guitar Hero* so well."

We all laugh. I'm elated by their reactions. It's exactly what I was hoping for. I feel closer to them than ever. See? You don't need a boyfriend when you've got great girlfriends.

"You guys want to hear another?" I ask.

"You bet," Katie says. She hops back up onto Marissa's bed.

"Yeah, encore!" Marissa cheers.

The three of them take out their cell phones and begin waving them back and forth, like fans at a concert who don't have cigarette lighters. Since the room isn't dark, the effect is somewhat limited, but I appreciate the gesture.

I don't want to play another love song, but I've already picked out a good second song.

"Here's one to girl power," I say as I launch into Gretchen Wilson's "Redneck Woman." The girls join in every time I get to the "hey ya'll" and "yee-haw" parts.

This is really fun.

And even better, cautious girl has just become a little less cautious....

## CHAPTER 32

It's the third weekend of spring semester, and I really couldn't ask for school to be going any better. Algebra is the only class I don't like—no surprise there. But one bad class out of five is a ratio I'll gladly take for the rest of my college career. History is okay, English and sociology are better than okay, and psychology is really fun. I think I may be heading for a major in psych, though I have no idea what I'll be able to do with it after I graduate. But that's a really long time from now, so no need to worry about it.

Playing guitar for my friends was a great idea. I feel closer to them than ever, and more importantly, I feel like a weight has been lifted from my shoulders. Keeping secrets is tough, even one as harmless as the fact that I play the guitar and sing a little. And did I mention it was really fun? Playing and having them sing along at the choruses? We're planning on doing it again soon.

Today though, I'm on my own. Marissa and Katie are spending the day with their guys, and Beth is fighting a cold. I've decided to head for the park. It's a beautiful day, mostly clear with temperatures in the fifties. There's no wind at all, and the bright sun makes it feel even warmer, especially after our recent cold spell. I'm wearing a yellow sweatshirt and black sports shorts. My white T-shirt protrudes a stylish three inches below my sweatshirt. I'm also wearing knee high sport socks with wide yellow and white stripes. The socks are a little "out there" for me, but they were a Christmas present from Marissa, who's continually trying to stretch my fashion sense.

On such a gorgeous winter weekend, I'm not surprised to find lots of people at the park, taking advantage of the great weather. There's a big soccer game going over on the field, as well as bunches of kids running around throwing Frisbees and footballs. There are even a couple of boats out on the lake.

More than a few guys out on the field are pretending it's summer by going shirtless. I guess all that exercise is keeping them plenty warm. I've already got my sweatshirt more than halfway unzipped, and I expect once I work up some more body heat I'll unzip it completely, if not take it off altogether.

At least half the grills in the picnic area have smoke curling up from them, and I can smell the tantalizing aromas of barbecued ribs and grilled beef as I pass. It's a good thing I had lunch just a little while ago, or I might find myself begging strangers for some of their food. The barbecue smells so good I'm tempted to do it anyway.

As I pass closer to the boat house, I see someone I recognize—James. I never took him up on his invitation to come by The Joint over the Christmas break, and I haven't seen him since that night Marissa, Andy and I went. He's wearing a light blue T-shirt over a long sleeve dark blue shirt and tan cargo shorts. It looks like he's getting ready to rent a boat.

I debate calling out to him, or going over to say hello. He's always been nice whenever I've seen him, and he doesn't seem to have any kind of agenda, unlike most guys. Of course, I've never been alone with him, so who knows? Maybe it's best if I just pass by and hope he doesn't notice me.

But what if he does see me? I'm getting pretty close to where he's standing—it would be hard to pretend I haven't seen him. I don't want him thinking I'm a snob, or that I don't like him.

This is exactly the kind of anxious, paranoid thinking I've been trying to avoid. See what guys can do to you, even when you're not dating? I wonder if I'll ever be done with it. Anyhow, the decision is taken out of my hands when James glances up and sees me. His mouth widens into a broad smile.

"Hey, Heather," he calls. "Long time no see."

I walk over to him. "Hi, James. Beautiful day, huh?"

"Sure is," he says. "Absolutely gorgeous."

"You renting a boat?" I ask.

"Yeah," he says. "It's one of my favorite ways to relax, but I don't get much chance to do it in the winter." He looks up at the sky. "Got to take advantage of days like this. Want to join me?"

Uh, oh. Now what do I do? I wasn't planning on having to deal with any kind of invite like that. Cautious girl rears her head—she doesn't want to get stuck out in a boat with a guy, even one as nice as James.

"Uh, no thanks," I say. "But thanks for the invite."

"C'mon," he says. "It'll be fun. You'll see."

"The water's awful cold," I say, trying to find a good reason to decline.

"Of course it's cold," he says, smiling. "It's the middle of winter. It's freezing cold. But we're going to be *on* the water, not in it."

"Boats have been known to tip over, you know," I say.

His grin widens. "Yes, indeed they have. But not when I'm in them. I've been rowing boats and paddling canoes since before I could walk, almost. I guarantee I'll keep you dry."

His manner is so warm and friendly, it's getting hard to resist. I haven't been out in a boat in forever, but few times I've done it, I've enjoyed it.

"Okay," I find myself saying. "What the heck. Let's do it."

"That's the spirit," he says. "We'll make a go-for-it girl out of you yet."

Five minutes later, James is holding me gently by the elbow and helping me into the back of a small metal rowboat. I feel the same current shoot through me as when he put his hand on my shoulder that night at The Joint. I wonder if he's found another one of those nerve bundle things. Somehow, I don't think so. Cautious girl begins to wonder if she's made a mistake accepting his invitation. But it's too late now.

James unties us from the dock and climbs easily into the boat, which scarcely rolls at all as he steps in. I guess he really does know what he's doing. He sits down on the middle seat and uses one of the oars to push us off from the dock. A moment later, he's got both oars in the locks and is rowing us smoothly out onto the lake.

"So, how's the new semester going?" James asks as he expertly pulls on the oars.

"Really good," I reply. "My classes are all pretty good, except for math, so I really can't complain. What about you?"

"I wish I could say the same," he says. "I've got two classes that are real bitches. Business Law and Advanced Accounting."

"I take it you're a business major, then?"

"Yeah." Somehow, he manages to shrug his shoulders without missing a beat in his rowing. "It's not that I love business, but it seems to be the most practical major, unless you're smart enough to do one of the computer ones."

I guess for a guy who's as determined as James to escape his home town, business really is a practical choice.

"If you could study anything you wanted, what would it be?" I ask.

"Environmental biology or psychology," he answers without hesitation. "I usually choose my electives from one of them."

"Psychology is my fave so far," I say. "I think I might end up a psych major, though I have no idea what I'll do with it."

"Yeah, that was my problem," James says. "I wanted to pick something that gives me the best chance of landing a good job when I graduate next year."

We've reached the middle of the lake. James lifts the oars smoothly from the water and expertly maneuvers them into the front of the boat. We glide forward for a few seconds before slowing to a dead stop. I can smell a faint, organic odor rising up from the lake bottom.

"How'd you get so good with boats?" I ask. "You must have had a lake or something near your home."

"Yeah, we had a big ol' reservoir only a couple miles from our house. My dad used to take us fishing all the time when we were young."

"Who's 'us'?" I ask. "You have brothers and sisters? You mentioned one brother in the army or something."

"Yeah, Tom. He's the only one. He's three years older than me." James grins. "Don't ever let him hear you say he's in the army—he's a Marine. Marines view the army as kind of like the minor leagues."

"You must be proud of him."

"I am. Very proud. He wanted to get away from home as bad as I did, so he enlisted right after high school. He's on his second tour in Afghanistan now."

"Wow, that must be scary. For you and for him."

"Scarier for me, I think. Tom loves it. Says he was born to be a Marine."

"Your mom and dad must really worry, though."

"My dad's not usually sober enough to worry about anything, except where his next drink is coming from," James says. There's an edge to his voice now. "And my mom died when I was eleven."

"Oh, I'm so sorry to hear that. My mom and dad can drive me crazy, but I wouldn't want to lose either one of them."

"My father was okay until mom died. I mean, he always drank some, but after she died, things really started going downhill."

"It must have been tough," I say.

"It was. But I'm out of there now. And it's much too beautiful out here to talk about that stuff."

He's right. It really is beautiful out here. And so peaceful, too. There's barely a ripple on the water, and the smooth surface reflects the rolling hills and blue sky almost like a mirror. There are only four or five other boats on the lake, none of them anywhere close to us, and the sounds from the park are no more than a faint whisper. I close my eyes and tilt my head back, letting the warm sunlight kiss my face. This is really nice. I'm glad I let James talk me into coming out here with him.

When I open my eyes, I find James staring at me.

"What are you looking at?" I ask, trying hard to sound like I'm teasing.

He smiles. "You look very peaceful. And totally relaxed."

"That's exactly how I feel. Relaxed and peaceful."

"I take it you're glad you came, then?"

I guess I'll have to add mind reading to his talents.

"Oh, yeah. Definitely," I say.


Time seems to both fly by and to stand still out on the lake. I'm not sure how that's possible, but that's how it feels. James and I talk non-stop for periods, and then lapse into silence for others. Both are comfortable. Nothing around us seems to change. The water remains still, the air warm. If it wasn't for the sun crawling slowly across the sky, it would be impossible to have any idea how long we've been floating out here.

Apparently James has a pretty good idea, though.

"We'd better head back," he says, stretching his arms above his head and then out to the sides. "It's been almost two hours."

I can't believe it's been two hours already. I check his wrists. He's not wearing a watch.

"How do you know how long it's been?" I ask. "Is that some backwoods nature boy trick?"

He laughs. "Shucks, t'ain't no trick a'tall, ma'am," he says in an exaggerated drawl that sounds like he just dragged himself out of some deep Appalachian valley. He holds his hand up with his thumb and finger spread about five inches apart. "When dat ol' sun moves hisself dis far 'cross da sky, den it's been 'bout two hours, sho 'nuff."

I can't help laughing.

"Wouldn't spect no city girl ta know dat, tho," he continues.

"Stop it!" I say, laughing harder and slapping his knee. "I apologize for the 'nature boy' comment."

James laughs and reaches into one of his pockets, pulling out his cell phone.

"I've got this set to vibrate on the hour," he explains. "It's three o'clock." He shoves the phone back into his pocket. "That's my 'backwoods' trick. I'll teach it to you sometime."

I laugh again. "Thanks, but I think I can figure that one out on my own."

James reaches behind him and grabs the oars, then slips them into the oarlocks and begins rowing us back toward shore. I find myself feeling really sorry our little adventure is coming to an end. But end it must, and a few moments later we're gliding up to the dock.

James judges our speed perfectly, and the boat edges up to the dock with only the slightest of thumps. He steps quickly out of the boat and ties it to a thick metal hook. I can't believe how gracefully he does it. Once again, the boat barely rolls. I get to my feet a lot more carefully—and a lot more clumsily, I'm afraid, because the boat is rocking pretty good now.

James reaches in and takes my hand to help me out.

"Here you are," he says as I step up onto the dock. "Safe and sound, and dry as a bone, as promised."

A feeling of disappointment grabs me when he lets go of my hand, but the smile on his face washes the disappointment away.

"That was really fun," I say. "Thank you."

"Any time," he says. "I had a great time, too."

We walk slowly down to the end of the dock, then turn left, strolling on the grass along the shore in the direction of the park entrance. There's a thin strip of dried mud between us and the water. I can hear the water softly lapping onto the mud.

"Hold on a second," James says.

He stoops and picks up a small flat stone from the dirt, hefting it in his hand and studying it for a moment like it's some kind of archeological treasure. I have no idea what he's doing. It looks pretty much like an ordinary rock to me.

Next thing I know, he bends slightly at the waist and whips the stone out over the water with an underhand sidearm motion. The stone skips four or five times atop the lake's surface before sinking out of sight.

"Wow," I say. "That's pretty good."

"Pretty good, yeah," he says, smiling. "But not quite good enough. My father used to tell us if we could get a rock to skip six times, we could make a wish that would come true. I only got five out of that one."

I bend down and pick up a rock of my own. "Let me try."

Before I can throw it, James stops me. He takes the rock from my hand.

"You need a flat one," he says. "This one's way too round. No way you can skip it."

He tosses it casually into the water and squats to find me a better rock. When he sees one he likes, he pries it out of the ground and brushes the mud from it.

"Try this one," he says. He wraps his thumb and index finger around the edge of the stone, like a backwards C. "Hold it like this."

He hands me the rock and I grip it the way he showed me. Trying to mimic how he threw his rock, I wing it out onto the lake. It hits the water with a splash and sinks without bouncing even once. Oh, well. I never claimed to be an athlete.

"No wishes for me, I guess."

"It takes practice," James says.

He picks up another stone and whips it out across the water. It skips so many times I lose count. Had to be at least six, though. I look at James and he's got his eyes closed and his head tilted slightly upward. I think he's making a wish.

"That was amazing," I say when he opens his eyes. "How many was it? I couldn't even count them."

"Seven," he says. "My record is nine. But seven is good enough for a wish."

"What did you wish for?"

"If I tell you, it won't come true. It's like blowing out the candles on a birthday cake. If you reveal the wish, you lose it." He smiles. "And I don't want to lose this one."

Dang. For some reason, I really want to know what he wished for. It will be almost a month before I find out.

We resume walking. Up ahead, the thick trunk of a fallen tree stretches almost to the water. The tree has been there a long time, and weather and people have long ago stripped the bark from the trunk, leaving a smooth, hard gray surface. When we reach the log, I can see scores of initials and hearts carved into the top and sides. Some of the carvings are old and weathered, others look fresh and sharp.

"Want to sit for a moment?" James asks.

"Sure. It's a pretty spot."

The tree makes a comfortable bench, just the right height for our feet to rest easily on the grass. From here, we've got an unblocked view across the lake to the hills beyond. Most of the trees on the hills are gray and bare, except for scattered clumps of dark green holly or mountain laurel bushes. The scene is desolate, but starkly beautiful nonetheless. The bright blue sky softens the barrenness, both above the hills and in the reflection on the water. On a gray, wintry day, I'm sure the desolation would be magnified.

It's starting to get a bit chilly as the sun creeps lower in the sky. The slanting rays don't hold the same warmth as the more direct ones did. I zip up my sweatshirt.

"Getting cold?" James asks.

"A little," I say.

He slides closer to me and puts his arm around my shoulders, like it's the most natural thing in the world.

The cold vanishes.

## CHAPTER 33

Flash forward. James and I have been dating for almost two months now, and it's been amazing. He's been so good for me, helping me gently out of my shell without ever pressuring me to do anything. I remember him saying he was going to make me more of a "go-for-it" girl. Well, I'm nowhere near that, but I'm definitely a lot less cautious and reserved than I was before we started going out. In a good way, I mean.

We've been back to the lake three times, and with the weather beginning to get warmer, I know we'll start going even more often. We think of the lake as "our place." James wants to teach me how to row, but I keep telling him I'm perfectly happy to sit and let him do all the work. Besides, I like watching the play of the muscles on his arms and under his shirt when he rows, though I haven't told him that, of course.

He's been teaching me how to skip rocks, which is fun. My arm is pretty weak and lame, but I can get at least three skips most of the time, and once I got five. I'm going to keep practicing, because if I can just add one more and do six, I'll get to make a wish. I remember Marissa saying the wishing star thing seldom works, but I know the rock skipping one does, because after James and I had been dating for a month, he finally told me what he wished for that first day at the lake. He wished for me and him to be together, as a couple. How sweet is that?

I've got my own wish all ready to go, but I can't tell you what it is, or it won't come true. And I really, really want it to come true. Now if I can just skip that darn rock six times!

Okay, enough about wishes. I've made a big decision. A really big decision. I've talked it over with Marissa, and she agrees I'm ready. Of course, she would probably have told me I was ready a month ago. But I wasn't, trust me. I'm not even positive I'm ready now, but we'll see. I told you I'm a lot less careful nowadays.

"Earth to Heather," Marissa says from across the room, drawing me out of my reverie.

I'm sitting at my desk, putting makeup on. At least, I was supposed to be putting makeup on, before my mind drifted off. I look at my reflection in the magnifying mirror in front of me. One eye is done—and looks pretty good, if I must say so myself—but the other one stares back at me all dull and forlorn. I've got my mascara brush in my hand, but I haven't touched the lashes on that eye. Hence the dull, forlorn look.

"Daydreaming?" Marissa asks. "Or having second thoughts?"

She's also been putting on makeup, but she's obviously done, because she's now twisted around in her chair, watching me.

"A little of both," I say. "But I'll take the daydream

any time. It's way more fun."

"I bet you would," Marissa says, grinning. "And I bet I know who you were dreaming about."

I smile back. "I was thinking about skipping rocks with James."

"Skipping rocks?" Marissa says. She shakes her head in a "what am I going to do with you" way. "That's my Heather, fantasizing about throwing rocks into a pond. You want to know what I dream about when I'm thinking of Andy?"

"No, please, no," I say. "I can only imagine. And I really don't want to imagine!"

Marissa laughs. "Okay, your loss. You might learn something, though."

"I've got enough on my mind, thank you. But thanks for the offer."

I lean closer to the mirror and start carefully applying mascara to my undone eye. I'm usually pretty casual with my makeup, but tonight's a big night, and I want it to look just right.

Even so, it doesn't take me long to finish. I'm not one of those girls who uses all kinds of fancy makeup tricks. A little blush, a touch of lip gloss, a bit of eye shadow and some mascara, and that's about it. Luckily, James likes the more natural look, and he's the only one who really counts.

I get up and check myself out in the full length mirror. I have to smile. I'm not sure the shy awkward girl who showed up here way back in September would even recognize the girl in the mirror. Not only is she better with makeup and clothes, but she seems to stand a bit straighter and has a more confident, less fearful look in her eyes. I owe most of that to Marissa, and more recently, to James. I'm so lucky to have both of them in my life.

I've chosen my outfit with the same thoughts in mind as with my makeup—easy, comfortable and moderately stylish. I'm wearing a variation of my old "hunting outfit," because my leggings and boots are about the most comfortable things I own, other than sweats and T's. Besides, I know James likes the way I look in them. I've paired the leggings with the ivory cable knit sweater I bought that same day at The Buff. My hair is down, but I've put a clip in either side to keep it from falling in front of my face. I'm finally starting to see what other people see when they tell me I'm cute. When Marissa or James use words like "gorgeous" I still cringe, but I've gotten comfortable with "cute," "pretty," and sometimes even "hot."

"You look great," Marissa says from behind me. "Perfect for tonight."

I'd probably say I look "pretty darn good," but I can handle "great," too.

"Thanks," I say. "You look pretty hot yourself."

Marissa can look very sexy when she wants to. What's really cool is she can look either trashy sexy or sophisticated sexy, depending on her mood and her plans. Tonight, she's leaning more toward the sophisticated side. She's wearing a short black skirt and knee high black leather boots with three inch heels. The combination makes her legs look longer than they really are. She's got on the same low cut gold lamé top she wore as part of her Halloween hooker costume, but because she's wearing it under a black short jacket with gray trim it doesn't look anywhere near as slutty as when she wore it with leather hot pants and fishnet stockings.

"I guess we're ready, then," Marissa says. "Let's go check on Katie and Beth."

We're going on a group date to The Joint tonight. Marissa and Katie will be with Andy and Grant, of course, and Beth will be with Brandon, a guy she's been dating for almost a month now. James is working, but he'll hang at our table as much as he can.

Marissa and I head down the hall toward Katie and Beth's room. Before we're halfway there, their door opens and Beth emerges. Katie appears a moment later. Beth smiles when she turns and sees us walking toward her.

"Perfect timing," she says. "You guys look great."

"Back at ya," Marissa says.

Beth is wearing a tight cotton dress with two inch wide powder blue and black stripes swirling diagonally around her body. Across her breasts, the stripes go in the opposite direction. The overall effect is to really show off her curves. She hasn't been dating Brandon all that long, so she's definitely still in the "dress to impress" stage. Her shoulders are bare, so she's got a black sweater draped over her arm for when it gets cool later in the evening. Katie has a long turquoise shirt over dark blue leggings. Instead of boots, she's wearing a cool pair of turquoise shoes.

Beth strikes a seductive pose and flips her hand through her hair. "The guys in The Joint are going to be bummed that we're all taken," she says. "Sucks for them. Good for us."

To keep things simple, we decided we would all walk together to The Joint and meet our guys there, rather than having them pick us up individually here at the dorm. I think Marissa suggested it so I wouldn't have to go alone. Afterwards, everyone can split up and go wherever they want. James is getting off early, so I won't be left stranded when everyone goes their separate ways.

It's almost the end of March, and the evening is quite pleasant. Daylight Savings started two weeks ago, so it's still light out when we leave the dorm, though the sun is almost gone. There's not a cloud in the sky, so the sunset provides no glorious colors tonight. Instead, the sky is slowing fading from a bright blue to a pale, washed out powder blue as the sun disappears. A bit of a breeze has risen from the west, and I wonder if we're in for a change in the weather. No matter, tonight is going to be fine, and that's what counts right now.

I'm enjoying our walk, laughing and joking with my friends, but as we get closer to The Joint I begin to feel nervous. I start to wonder if my decision is a smart one, or if it's still too soon. I suppose I can always change my mind—that's a woman's prerogative, right? I picture James' handsome face. Why would I want to change my mind? Because the first time is always scary, that's why.

I must have unconsciously slowed my pace, because all of a sudden my three friends are several yards in front of me.

Marissa is the first to notice. She stops and turns back toward me, a questioning look on her face.

"You okay, Heather?" she asks.

I pick up my pace. "Yeah, sorry," I say. "I was just

thinking. I guess I got distracted."

"Thinking? Or worrying?" Marissa asks. She knows me all too well.

"A little of both," I admit.

"You're going to be fine," Marissa says. "There's nothing to worry about."

I sure hope she's right.

## CHAPTER 34

When we get to The Joint, Andy and Brandon are already inside. They're sitting pretty close to the front, just to the right of center, at three tables James has pushed together for us. The guys give Marissa and Beth hugs and say hello to me and Katie. James is on the other side of the room talking to one of the waiters, but I catch his eye and he smiles and waves.

I take a seat by the end of the table, so James will be able to sit next to me on the end whenever he can get away from his duties. Marissa sits on my left, where she can provide maximum support and distraction. Andy takes the chair next to her, then come Brandon and Beth, with Katie down at the far end, an empty seat next to her for Grant, who arrives just a few minutes later.

James finally manages to break away and comes by to say hello.

"Now this is what I call a good-looking group," he says, smiling. He leans down and gives me a quick kiss on the lips. "Especially you," he whispers in my ear before straightening up.

The kiss and the comment serve to raise the

temperature in the room a few degrees. I am one happy girl—still nervous, but happy.

"I'll be back soon," James says. He turns and heads toward the front doorway.

As I watch him weave his way among the tables, I decide that he looks equally good coming or going. I wonder if Marissa, Katie and Beth also think their guy is the best looking guy in the room. They probably do. They'd all be wrong, of course, but it's good if they think that way.

Our waiter arrives a moment later. I'm not sure how well my stomach will handle solid food right now, so I order a strawberry banana smoothie instead. The rest of my friends all order real food, and our waiter scurries away toward the kitchen.

Our order is so large he has to make three trips to our table to bring all the food. When he puts down the last of the dishes, there is still no smoothie for me. Before I can say anything, James is standing next to me, a big pink smoothie in his hand.

"I had them put extra strawberries in it," he says as he places the tall glass in front of me. He knows I love strawberries. He's always doing little things like that for me.

"Thanks," I say. I take a quick sip. "It's delicious."

James reaches down and gives my hand a quick squeeze. "I'll be back as soon as I can," he says. And away he goes.

Marissa has gotten fries to go with her burger, and they look and smell awfully good. She catches me eyeing them and tells me to take a few, so I do. The fries taste almost as good as my smoothie, so I'm pretty well set.

I'm starting to feel more nervous again. I wish James was sitting here next to me, rather than working, but if he didn't work here we wouldn't be getting the special treatment we're getting tonight, so I don't really mind. As soon as everyone's done eating, he'll be able to spend more time here with me. And I'm *really* grateful for the special treatment I'll be getting in just a little while.

Our table is among the last to finish eating, and our waiter has barely cleared our dishes away when the MC bounces up onto the stage.

"Welcome, ladies and gentlemen, to open mic night at The Joint." The usual cheers follow his greeting. "We're going to start things off a little differently tonight. We've had a special request, and since it's from someone who's a close friend of a member of The Joint family, we've cheerfully agreed."

My stomach is beginning to churn. Where's James? I need him here right now, in more ways than one. I look toward the employee break room and see him emerging through the doorway. He smiles, and I immediately feel a little bit better.

"Most of you know we usually begin with Tony Phillips," the MC continues. He waits while another flurry of cheers quiets down. "Tony is here tonight, and he'll be performing for you in just a bit."

Tony is sitting up front to the left, and he smiles and waves his hand to the crowd as they applaud him.

"But before we get to Tony, we've got a special guest for you."

James has made it to our table and takes the seat next

to me. He's brought my guitar, which has been waiting safely in the break room.

I'm really nervous now. My hands are shaking as James hands me my guitar. The special guest the MC is talking about is me. I had James ask if I could perform first, so I'd have less chance to chicken out or be intimidated by the other performers. Now I wish I hadn't requested the favor. Maybe I should have gone last, or after that crummy comedian, if he's here. Yeah, that might have been better. Anything but first.

Marissa knows how I'm feeling. She lays her hand gently on my forearm.

"You can do this, Heather," she says. "I know you can. You'll be great."

I wish I shared her confidence. How did I get myself into this? I wonder if it's too late to change my mind. I'm about to do just that.

"Our first guest will be performing tonight for the first time anywhere," the MC says. "We're thrilled she chose The Joint for her debut. Give it up for Heather!"

Oh god, what have I gotten myself into? I'm frozen in my seat. That's probably a good thing, because if I try to stand, I don't think my legs will support me. James gets up and takes my hand. He gently pulls me from my seat and walks me up to the stage. He gives my hand a firm squeeze before returning to his seat.

I sit down and the MC lowers the microphone for me.

A moment later, I'm all alone on stage. My heart is racing and my mouth is dry. How am I ever going to sing? I look at James. He's smiling warmly up at me. He doesn't know it yet, but this is my present to him.

I close my eyes, trying to wipe away everything but the feel of my guitar on my lap. I'm in my room, playing by myself, the way I've done a thousand times before. I begin strumming the strings. I've picked the perfect song, and I've been practicing it for weeks. It's one of Taylor Swift's, of course, because who does love better than Taylor? And this one almost could have been written specifically for me and James.

I play the introductory chords several times—more than I'm supposed to. I need to start singing soon, or I may never start. Not to mention I could get booed off the stage. Thank goodness the opening words are so simple—just a string of "oh's" is all. I begin singing.

There's no turning back now. But that doesn't mean I have to open my eyes yet. As long as I keep them closed, I'm alone in my room. I'll open them when the time is right.

I'm singing about being down by the lake, and I ad lib a line about skipping rocks on the water. The words come easily to me—why shouldn't they? They're my story. I reach the key line in the whole song and I open my eyes, fastening them on James' face. I'm singing to him. There's no one else in the room.

A huge smile lights up his face. He's looking at me with more love than I ever thought I would find. Fairy tales can come true, I think as I sing to him that he is far and away the best thing I've ever had in my life.

He truly is. The very best thing. And he's mine.

# ABOUT THE AUTHOR

**Scott Prussing** was born in New Jersey, but was smart enough to move to beautiful San Diego as soon as he received his Master's degree in psychology from Yale University. In addition to *Mine: A Love Story*, Scott is the author of the paranormal romance Blue Fire Saga (*Breathless, Deathless* and *Helpless*). In addition to writing, Scott enjoys going to the movies (not renting!), riding his bicycle near the beach, reading all kinds of books, hiking and golf. He is one of the few remaining people in the United States without a cell phone.

Contact Scott and learn all about his books at
www.scottprussing.com